ZUBAIDA'S WINDOW

Women Writing the Middle East

Baghdad Burning: Girl Blog from Iraq
by Riverbend

Baghdad Burning II: More Girl Blog from Iraq
by Riverbend

Children of the New World
by Assia Djebar

Harem Years: The Memoirs of an Egyptian Feminist
by Huda Shaarawi

The Loved Ones: A Modern Arabic Novel
by Alia Mamdouh

Naphtalene
by Alia Mamdouh

On Shifting Ground: Muslim Women in the Global Era
Edited by Fereshteh Nouraie-Simone

Touba and the Meaning of Night
by Shahrnush Parsipur

Women Without Men
by Shahrnush Parsipur

ZUBAIDA'S WINDOW

A NOVEL OF IRAQI EXILE

IQBAL AL-QAZWINI

Translated from the Arabic
by Azza El Kholy and Amira Nowaira

Afterword by Nadje Al-Ali

The Feminist Press
at the City University of New York
New York

Published in 2008 by The Feminist Press at the City University of New York
The Graduate Center, 365 Fifth Avenue, Suite 5406, New York, NY 10016
www.feministpress.org

Text copyright © 2006 by Iqbal Al-Qazwini
Translation copyright © 2008 by Azza El Kholy and Amira Nowaira
Afterword copyright © 2008 by Nadje Al-Ali

Originally published in 2006 in Arabic by Azminah under the title *Mamarrat as-Sukoon*.

Library of Congress Cataloging-in-Publication Data
Al-Qazwini, Iqbal.
Zubaida's window : a novel of Iraqi exile / by Iqbal Al-Qazwini ; translated from
the Arabic by Azza El Kholy and Amira Nowaira ; afterword by Nadje Al-Ali.
p. cm.
ISBN 978-1-55861-572-4 (trade cloth)
I. El Kholy, Azza. II. Nowaira, Amira. III. Title.
PJ7958.A98Z445 2008
892.7'36—dc22
2007033833

This publication was made possible, in part, by public funds from the New York
State Council on the Arts, a state agency, and the National Endowment for
the Arts.

Text and cover design by Lisa Force

12 11 10 09 08   5 4 3 2 1

CHAPTER ONE

At dawn, the fighter planes coming from their bases in the warm Arabian Gulf discharge their first hot and heavy loads. The armies move forward, tanks rolling, guns spewing fire. Palm trees burn, houses collapse, birds scatter, and Baghdad wakens to doomsday. Planes race with tanks to comb the area and dispel doubts that war has come. Soldiers speak through microphones attached to their helmets. They give signals, receive instructions, and open fire. People die. Don't worry, soldier, no law will ever convict you! The laws of war say you must kill before you are killed. No sound except planes in the sky, and on the ground the rumble of tanks. On radio and television, broadcasters crowd the air waves.

Coalition forces bombard the port of Umm Qasar in the south of Iraq. Signs of sporadic resistance begin to appear throughout the harbor. Coalition forces comb the area.

It seems to Zubaida that the whole world has gathered in Iraq, that nothing exists outside its borders. Pictures of death unroll on the TV screen as she watches, feeling confused about whether she should continue watching. She feels rather dizzy, her breathing becomes increasingly irregular. She longs for some fresh air to clear her smoke-choked lungs. She opens the door of the sitting room which leads to the balcony on the eighth floor of her building. On a wooden bench shaped like a half bed she collapses. Nearby, the large iron satellite dish reels as if drunk, while the noise of fighter planes and missiles continues blasting out of the TV, which she has left switched on in the sitting room.

On her balcony, she imagines that huge fighter planes are approaching from the distant horizon and entering the satellite dish through its wires. Planes drift across the open door of the balcony into her apartment, and become transformed into small toys. Still, the noises coming from the television grant them a destructive power. She watches people screaming, children escaping out of the three eyes of the satellite dish to float away skyward as in a dream. Some of them don't manage to fly. They fall down on the smooth shiny surface of the dish. After several desperate attempts, they plunge down from the eighth floor.

From the balcony of her apartment in a city still strange to her, she watches the scene so attentively that she moves closer to the balcony railings and looks down. For a moment, she looks for the children whose bodies seem to her to have hit the pavement, drenched with spring rain.

In front of her eyes, Baghdad is being destroyed one stone after the next. The planes are not responsible. They simply burn away the traces of destruction begun decades earlier. They have come to get rid of the evidence of a hidden plan to destroy her country. This was the place she had always dreamed of living in, running away from, and returning to. That it should be stripped of its symbols of ancient history and its identity! She does not know, nor can she find the link that binds her to those faces, wavering between cruelty and kindness, faces scorched by the sun while being driven away to be offered as clandestine sacrifices. She is absorbed in the terrified faces, the indifferent eyes, and the languid foreheads. She walks back and forth in the room, goes out onto the balcony, then comes back to watch what is happening, and sinks into emptiness. She stops to feel time, while the world outside shrinks into moving pictures, tracking the tanks roaming the streets of a ghost city. All she can see is artillery fire blending with the black belt of burning oil encircling the besieged city with rivers of blackness.

That place once represented for her an uneasy dream, vacillating between wakefulness and sleep, between audacity and fear, between the possible and the impossible. That is the place she has been longing for. It burns before her eyes and almost disappears in the fire. She sees that place as a tongue of flame moving out of the screen and settling in the sitting room. The blazing fire unites with her blazing soul. Iraqi television at the last gasp tries to rouse the same people it has helped crush, with the words of a new song invoking Ali, the father of Hassan and Al-Hussein, lying dead in his grave for more than a thousand years, to save the homeland. She shudders. Her body trembles as she imagines herself in the middle of a raging ocean. The air is pregnant with the odors of fear and incense. Terrified as she is, she seems to hear the wailing of bereaved mothers. With an invisible human choir, she repeats: "Peace on you, my absent homeland. Peace on you, fearful bird."

Zubaida sinks into a cloud of grief and smoke, enveloped by the din of destruction exploding on the screen. Dazed and in tears, she switches off the television. Her mixed feelings well up. She recognizes how weak and abject the ruler is. But at the same time, she knows there is a missing truth that should be kept hidden and unknown so that her Iraq can be destroyed. She also remembers thousands of people forced out of their lands, deported on trucks, a trembling cargo to be disgorged on mined territory near the border with Iran. In her soul the living dreams

3

reemerge, once buried with the dreamers in mountains and deserts during tribal pogroms, perpetrated in silence and without any qualms. She feels the nerve gas quietly playing with the plaits of the little blond girl, who remains asleep on the step before the front door of her house. The columns of silent soldiers march in her imagination, driven to wars from which they will not return.

A hand reaches out. A head tries to wrench itself out of a burning tank. An injured Iraqi soldier gathers the strength to pull himself out and find refuge on the ground. Foreign snipers in the distance watch him, amused. They wait until their quarry feels safe; then they shoot. Between the satellite pictures and the golden domes, the sky rages with a sand storm as red as blood. Satellite correspondents transmit fresh news, and Zubaida smells the odor of spilt blood and drinks bitter tea.

She follows the movements of an elderly woman whose long dusty black *abaya* slides a little off her head, revealing gray hair, which she has wrapped hastily in a white head-scarf. She heads nowhere. She crosses the street, then goes back as though searching in vain for her house. Noticing her, the TV reporter comes closer and asks a question. But she does not seem to hear him. She looks distracted, almost in a state of amnesia, or rather like a person just coming out of a coma, not knowing where she is. She keeps moving back and forth around the area like someone possessed; then she disappears from the frame. Zubaida weeps over the birds, exhausted from constant flight, besieged and suffocated by the smoke, suspended between earth and sky. In the deserted southern city, a very old man walks heavily with the help of a stick. A strange smile appears on his face; he seems indifferent to the fires raging around him. Zubaida sticks her head over the balcony and asks him about the people who have disappeared. He tells her as he continues walking: "Are you asking about someone in particular?"

"No, not exactly! But where are all the people? Where have they gone?"

"They're gone! No one is left!"

"Gone where?"

"They're fine, all gone the way they chose."

The piercing sounds of air-raid sirens rouse her. She comes out of the TV screen.

In Berlin, at such an immense distance from Baghdad, Zubaida stays up all night, alone, watching the war and listening to the sounds of explosions in her homeland. In the morning, on the adjacent balcony to the left, a fat man in a good mood waters the colorful potted flowers arranged tidily along the balcony rail. When he sees her, he greets her and asks timidly, as though apologizing in advance for posing a useless question: "Excuse me! Haven't you told me some time ago that you come from Iran?"

"No, sir. I'm from Iraq."

Apologetically, he says: "Yes, yes, from over there! The land of *One Thousand and One Nights*! Iran!"

"It's Iraq, sir, that's the land of *One Thousand and One Nights*, and not Iran!"

"Yes, yes. Please forgive me, all the names of these countries of yours are so similar! Iraq is written exactly like Iran in our language with the exception of the last letter.

"European countries are suffocating with all these newcomers. They're not tourists who bring money into Europe. They often leave their rich countries and come here for political and sometimes economic reasons. They arrive here and not only receive benefits as political refugees but also rob shops and homes. As soon as a German forgets to lock up his bike, he watches it moving off, ridden by an immigrant coming from such countries. . . ."

She hears, as he does, the sounds of explosions coming from

the TV set. He continues: "The explosions are in Iran, and we can hear them here in Berlin."

"You mean Iraq, sir!"

"Yes, yes. Iraq! Those poor kids."

Zubaida is almost on the verge of jumping out of the eighth-floor balcony, as he continues watering the potted flowers, prattling disjointedly about politics, his problems with the neighbors, and with the building's elevator, mixing the reasonable and the absurd. She imagines herself standing on the balcony rail and jumping from the eighth floor. But instead of falling to the ground, she flies skyward, her body crashing against one of those planes. Her imagination shifts among the artillery fire, the noise of planes, and the prattling of a neighbor who is not completely aware of what he is saying, all in a country where she feels alien. Still, she carries German identity papers and a passport and feels grateful for that bit of false security. She waits uneasily for the neighbor to finish watering his plants so that she can go inside. But he changes the topic: "There's a bee that comes here every day and looks at this big vase. If it could find its friend, it would stay with it. Otherwise, it would go back. Life is sometimes bizarre. They're still bombing your city, aren't they? What a pity!"

"Yes, sir." She thinks, "It is happening here in my soul, too. They're bombing my memory."

The mind, or the remnants thereof, develops an amazing mechanism so that the pulse continues to beat, the lungs to breathe, the eyes to see, the stomach to feel hunger, the mouth to feel thirst, and the body to fall asleep out of exhaustion. Zubaida's mind also keeps her from falling into madness. It helps her stay on the edge, walking precariously on a rope stretched across a bottomless abyss, keeping a perilous balance.

Three lives reside within her soul. She ran away from the first life but hopes to return. In East Germany she settled into a second life and for years has tasted the cruelty of being a stranger. Here she feels her first life has vanished, turned into a lost period in a world not her own. The third life is the one she yearns for but can never reach. Only in one place can she dream, even of impossibilities. On her way to the first dream, she gets lost and finds new dreams and an unavoidable hell. How difficult it is to pull one's memories along, in all their detail! And how heavy they are, although they seem to be no more than hot blue air! This is how she imagines them. These memories dwell deep in her soul, and cannot be gathered in one place, nor collected into a single bundle of clothing to be stacked away on the shelf of an old doorless cupboard. She has often felt unable to rid herself of this loaded dream. She has felt it dragging her along, firmly holding her by her hair and forcing her to follow its movements. Living in a present that offers her absolutely nothing, she gives full rein to an old dream that she feels comfortable pursuing. She steps onto a road that happens to be there, driven toward a force she can no longer resist. When she senses the shrinking of her body as it divides and subdivides, she rushes toward the mirror, trying to reassure herself that she still has the viable appearance of a unique human being, and that she has not vanished completely. She spends the following days watching the war at a distance, measuring time between the balcony and the window.

Zubaida does not know the exact moment when these memories begin to take the shape of some dramatic events on a stage, performed before her eyes, disappearing, then reappearing. Something conjures up these events and invites the past to surge in, at times suddenly, and at other times as if according to plan. The aroma of earth may spur the events lying dormant in the closet of her spirit. Her memories may feel caressed by the sounds of rain falling on strange grass, or tickling the rustling leaves, or even by a ray of light between the shutters of a window, or the color of a wall. These memories, awakened, walk with her and disturb her freedom. Although at first she feared the random release of memories, now she misses their embrace.

She does not care any more how many years are still to come! She recognizes that she lives on an imaginary sustenance that will always stay with her. Once she had had to stop at a difficult crossroads where she had lost her direction and could not find her way out. Today she looks in vain for a viable way in. Today, she gets lost amid the crowded archways, a child who has never grown up. In her dreams, languages, faces, places, and seasons blend, so there is snowfall in the summer of Baghdad and a July sunshine on the October mornings of cold Berlin. As she awakens and realizes that the circle is still closing in on her, she also understands that fate has its own calculations and arrangements.

Starting all over again, she dresses the bleeding wounds and counts the scars. Then she jumps up, closes the gate of the past, and opens a hole that reveals an indistinct light. She imagines that the light is coming toward her. Zubaida, who walks out of an old photo album, dyes her hair, and sits on the balcony of a strange city, watching the passersby who roam the streets in the dead of the night, accompanied by their obedient dogs. When the morning appears on the balcony, she leaves and heads toward a day clamoring for stillness and waiting. She opens the closet of memory, throws away all that has clung to it, and reaches its farthest corners to drag out the contents of a heavy box. She holds the events, the photos, the dead, the semi-dead, the living, the semi-living, the indifferent, the travelers without destinations, those who cry tearlessly and those who laugh meaninglessly. She takes hold of many failures and disappointments, and throws them onto the floor where they collect at her feet. She leaves the floor full of chaotic litter and treasures, and goes to the kitchen to place her head beneath the cold water tap. Her head soaking wet, she drinks water from her palms. Turning off the water, she returns to the confused mound of her life, collapsing in front of the rubble, as the drops of water fall from her hair onto the dry grass of her life, evoking the aroma of an ancient dream. She bares her arms and begins the task of arranging.

She spreads her memories on the carpet of the room, drying the water on the scenes spread out around her. She sits upright, drawing a deep breath. She feels a piercing pain in her chest as she bends over a period she cannot sort out. She tries to stand, leaning on boxes filled with imaginings. As her hands slide through the emptiness, she loses her balance and returns to the floor. She stays in this position until she falls asleep. A young man's spirit emerges from the debris beside her and visits her dream. She reaches out to hold him, but he turns away and disappears. Transfixed and unable to catch up with him, she wails. Waking from her reverie, she feels suffocated. She tries to escape to the balcony, but she trips over the remains of a soul scattered among the debris of her life. She tramples hard on an absence, opening an old injury. Always she feels guilty when he appears. Here he is once again, emerging from her memories, remaining at a distance, silently blaming her.

This evening, the whole past comes back to her, strong, mighty, and young. She tries in vain to recall the cadence of his young voice. She is not sure whether her dream is an old repeated one or a new one: An unknown person hands her an envelope with her name on it. When she tries to read the letter, she cannot decipher a single word, even though the writing is perfectly legible. She recognizes that she is dreaming and that she has to decode the secret of the dearly loved letter quickly. She manages to read only one word, which she utters out loud in a tranquil voice in order to remember it when she wakes up. The words falter across the lines of the letter, and the dream time passes quickly. She fears the illusion may evaporate, not knowing for sure whether she was to feel happy or sad about a letter coming in the dream. Is it possible that even from the grave, he can toy with her yearnings and her dreams? Or has sleep released old memories and hopes and given them full rein to do as they please?

When she used to tell him that she was planning to leave on a certain day, heading far away, he'd keep very quiet. He would then say abruptly: "We'll always stay here together." He knew he had deep roots there, roots too deep to cut or dig up. His roots will always remain with her like eternal threads. But her deep desire to leave never weakened. She never felt a part of the world around her, though she was unable to express her feelings even to him. Lonely now, she cries, still hearing his words ringing in her ears: "We'll always stay here together." But she simply left without even looking back, to find herself in one half of a cold city, whose other half was encircled by electrified wire and iron helmets, planted by an iron regime in the middle of the dynamic West. She became a prisoner in this city.

On the day the plane landed at the end of April, the sun did not appear. The sky was gray with scattered drops of water. She waited a whole week for the sun to appear, but it did not, and the sky remained overcast. On the first of May, she saw a parade of red flags. It was like a silent movie into which color was forced, superimposed. The whole thing looked fake and voiceless. She saw people moving with a terrifyingly mechanical gait, marching in an organized, lifeless procession in front of a platform, where overweight bodies stood wearing hats and waving to the marching human procession. Attendants hoisted black umbrellas over the heads of the fat bodies. Everything was over in a few hours. Every step had been studied, every movement perfected. The crowd disappeared quietly, but the small red paper flags remained scattered all over the square, and along the sides of the wide road. This was lesson number one in the funeral procession of internationalism.

For Zubaida, dilapidated statues collapsed one after the other. Tearless, she cleared the splinters falling from her head. It was eight o'clock in the evening during the first week of her stay in a one-room apartment in the middle of Berlin's split heart. This was the time when all the streets of the city fell asleep. She heard the sounds of shootings at the nearby wall, referred to as the border or the inspection point for entry into the American sector in the western part of Berlin. A Soviet soldier had tried to escape in his military vehicle. When he failed, however, he turned hysterical and began shooting his automatic weapon at the people around. He was surrounded and killed. The image of the smashed glass splattered with dried blood on the asphalt of the street would not leave Zubaida's mind for years to come. In the stillness of the first evenings of her stay, she got used to the sounds of shooting in the death zone, the forbidden area in the besieged city. She did not at first comprehend the depths of suffering of those on whose land she was living until she had left naïveté behind to enter the solitary confinement of awareness. During endless nights, and before she goes to bed, she ties down the chair for fear it might walk away, admonishes the curtains to stop chattering, implores the books to remain on the shelves, then opens her arms to the little death. She closes the gates of the present behind her and sinks into an old dream.

An explosion takes place at a press office. The cameramen come out, all soaking in blood, holding their cameras in their hands and running. One of them screams because his colleague has fallen dead. Others carry the injured and deposit them in their private cars and drive off.

The war she watches on television today is the same as, or an extension of, the previous one that broke out on the Iranian front. The soldiers who die today are the same soldiers who died yesterday, but are dying one more time. They die, then come back to life to die once again. Then the cycle begins again until the spark of life has completely disappeared. The fear that overtook her yesterday at a meaningless war is the same fear she feels today, as she watches the destruction of the land on the screen.

She tries to imagine the extent of the destruction encompassing the whole country. The mail which she fears today, carrying nothing but messages of disappointments, is the same mail she feared yesterday. She looks at the letters spread out before her, not wishing to open them, and remembers the day the mail brought her a letter from both her brother, Ahmed, and the one she called "The Warbling Nightingale," her relative Tahseen, in Amman. The letter told her that they had both arrived in Amman and were looking for somewhere to stay. They were fleeing the infernal might of the war with Iran, which had stopped all of life's activities. People were driven to the war and offered as fodder to its ravenous fires that forever demanded more. Ahmed had been offered a position as a teacher of music in Tunisia, and he was planning to accept it. Then Tahseen, The Warbling Nightingale, had obtained a training course in East Germany, which he took advantage of in order to run away. Their letter contained an oblique reference to the loss of contact with her soldier brother stationed at the war front.

That war had produced a bitter reality and some weird tales. A father killed his son because his son had run away from the battlefront. When the father told the dictator about the incident, he, the murderer father, received a sum of money and a Mercedes, gifts from the dictator. The media made a film about this father and named him "friend of the leader."

In the photos of the soldiers lurking behind the ramparts today, she can see a picture of her brother in a previous war on the front with Iran. She places her hands over her face and lets her mind wander, remembering her soldier brother. She sees him lying in a ditch as the sounds of artillery come from every direction. She imagines him at the moment when his unit retreated without relaying to him the retreat order and leaving him completely alone. She wishes he had been taken prisoner.

Dear God! Preserve our country! Dear God! Preserve our people from destruction!

Zubaida murmurs and weeps over her brother, the dreamy child. She sees him before her with a lock of hair falling on his forehead. He would push it back even if sleeping in a ditch, then would crawl through tunnels amid the din of artillery and the blazing fires. She remembers how she imagined him then, thirsty and pleading with friends for a drop of water. She imagines him hungry and dreaming of a crust of bread. Was it possible that he, who had always been immensely fond of bathing, could stay at the front without any water touching his body? She still remembers her monologue as she read the letter that evening so long ago. She talked to herself then as though she were addressing him: "Promise you'll stay alive so I can see you. Please don't die or kill. You don't know what killing is. Shoot into the air and never aim at any human being; otherwise our father would be distressed. He was a man without any spite. Promise me you will keep your word and stay alive. I want you alive, because I love seeing you. How is it that you grew up and carried a gun without my knowing it? I had hoped to see you as a young man going out of the house dressed in your blue shirt, attracting all the young women of the neighborhood."

She drowns in the minutiae of boredom and gets lost in mazes of bitterness, without power, youthfulness, and color. She hates to run away from her bewilderment by embracing a philosophy of hateful, false justification. When the evening descends, as alien and friendless as she, the illusions become her only refuge. But for how long? How she hates the yard on which her bedroom window opens! How she hates the lights coming out of windows in the faded building opposite, which she sees every morning when she opens the curtains! How many desolate nights will bear down on her chest as she sits on wooden benches, the color of earth, in deserted train stations that have no doors through which to leave. But no train arrives to take her away. Emptiness has never been as terrifying as it is now. Like the hands of the clock, helpless and shackled, she turns the dial and returns to the starting point. Like the hands of a clock, she is caught in a circular trap, turning around and around without any hope of salvation.

She writes to friends. When friends are not there, she invents them. She discusses with one of them the idea of leaving for good, or simply traveling. She writes hundreds of letters, sends a number of them, and tries to share her thoughts and feelings of unbearable restlessness with one of them. She receives a letter telling her that departure is from the self and traveling is for the self, in the hope of rediscovering the self and asking for forgiveness. These thoughts perplex her, since they only accentuate the silence. Will the remaining years of her life be sufficient for an old cart pulled by exhausted horses?

The rain fell nonstop last night. It kept thumping against her window until she fell asleep out of sheer exhaustion. The noise of the following morning coming from outside disappears slowly, and the sun vanishes quietly behind the tall gray buildings. For Zubaida, the whole universe seems devoid of people. Overwhelmed by an overriding sense of loss, she feels her body cringe as she imagines herself all alone in the world, all the creatures having deserted the earth for another universe and forgotten to take her along with them. From the dim passage, she looks in amazement at her bedroom, which seems to her to be swimming in a sea of light. She enters and stands to one side, attracted by her mother's sad face which appears suddenly on the other shore, then floats in the air. Zubaida jumps into the sea of light, resisting feelings of fear and emptiness overwhelming every cell in her body, and tries to swim toward the other side. Before getting there, her mother's face disappears as suddenly as it has appeared. Zubaida drowns in surges of light that drag her down to the bottom.

She has the urge to walk the familiar but unknown streets of the city. She puts on her coat, takes her umbrella, and leaves the apartment. She stands alone at the end of the street. Only cars pass in front of her in the early darkness of the city. She sees nobody walking. She decides to keep wandering and stands at a bus stop. When the bus arrives, she gets on it, only to get off it when she sees people walking about. She walks aimlessly, indifferent to the elegant shop windows, which mean absolutely nothing to her in her total isolation. Cafés are overcrowded, but nobody sits alone, for where is the pleasure in sipping a cup of coffee alone and then going back home? At a café, she chooses a chair outside and orders tea with a slice of lemon. She is aware that some people are scrutinizing her, or so it seems. She looks at her watch, then at the street, in the hope of hinting to the café customers that she has a date and is expecting someone. Loud music blares out of the small amplifiers fixed at the corners of the café, merging with the noises of football fans watching a match on a TV screen fixed to the wall. She digs into her pocket, pays the bill for the tea, and leaves. Walking on the streets of the city, she sees a group of young people joyfully singing some kind of anthem. She is not quite sure whether they are celebrating the victory of a team competing for the European Cup or whether they are simply singing and having fun. She asks herself: Do I have any connections to this world?

She finds herself in her apartment, not knowing which bus she took or how long she has walked to get there. When she enters her apartment, she feels at home. She makes a cup of tea, which seems to taste totally different. At this moment, she feels completely free. But she knows that her feelings of freedom or enslavement are part of her being in a strange place, surrounded by strange people. She asks herself why she keeps repeating this test, going out and trying to feel at home, since she knows she will get the same results. Nothing will change. Nothing. Nothing here can bring back joy to her soul.

Run away, Zubaida. You are a fugitive here, a fugitive in

every sense of the word, a fugitive from the neighbor who will never stop asking about when you plan to go home, as though your presence were a burden to him. He likes you a lot and enjoys talking to you when he finds you on the balcony. But your features and hair color always remind him that you are an alien plant in his soil. Run away, Zubaida. You are not wanted here. The neighbor is not so neighborly, and the friend is not so friendly. The neighbor should be a person who is close to you in spirit rather than in location. At home, an old saying goes, "Your neighbor, then your neighbor, then your neighbor, and then your brother." There is also another that goes, "Choose your neighbor before you choose your home, and choose your companion before the road you take." Such sayings used to sound meaningless to her. How we made fun of them, laughed at them, replaced them with political slogans, and finally left them on the shelves of the forgotten! Now, they have become meaningful. It was a mistake to replace feelings with political slogans, and we have been forced to bear the consequences. You knew where the fault lay, but you could not free yourself of it except when it was too late. Run, Zubaida, run! Can you do it? It's up to you, for you'll be the one to suffer the consequences. You alone! So when will you make up your mind?

The next day brings a host of trivialities including a compulsory visit to the labor office, which is one of the great achievements of neocapitalism. She sits in a long passage, scrutinizing the lifeless faces before her. She knows she will accomplish nothing, but she is indifferent about the effort she will expend. In the beginning, she welcomed the new burden, for it had seemed to bring freedom. The trivialities of another day pass, ending meaninglessly. In the dead of night, she gets out of bed, picks her way through the darkness, stumbling toward the light switch. She presses it, and the blaring light declares it is two o'clock in the morning. Time hangs in the corridor of her apartment on a clothes hook near her black coat. Time, which makes all creatures grow old, is itself sleeping on a hook, like a little bat that awakens her with its snores. She stands at the door of her room and looks at the corridor, partially illuminated by the light coming from her room. She stares from a distance at sleeping Time and remembers last night's, and every night's, dreams.

In this particular dream, she looks for his grave in a strange land, always at sunset. She sees herself searching, wavering between despair and hope, and thinking of Time passing like lightning and removing the remnants of light. In the dream, she bemoans her bewilderment. How could she forget his burial place? How can her memory fail her? She is tossed about by the dream, still searching and getting lost in this strange place, until she decides to wake up and leave the dream. Fully awake, she feels the smoke of sadness seep into the farthest recesses of her soul. She feels too paralyzed to get up. Why does the dream remove the features, and why can't she remember the color of his eyes? Why do the details escape her when she has believed they were engraved in her mind? Is this the bliss of forgetfulness or is it the effect of Time, the creature hanging on the hook?

She leaves the room, walks along the corridor, switches on the light, then lifts Time off the hook. She takes it to the bathroom, dumps it into the toilet, and flushes. Back in bed she decides to ignore it, although she is pretty certain that it will come back, concealing itself in some place, perhaps a closet. It may even hide in her handbag, and she will have to carry it along wherever she goes. During the long nights of winter in foreign parts, the nightmare enters the dream, merges with it, seeps into the brain grooves filled with dust, ghosts, and empty suitcases waiting for other gray, arid mornings.

CHAPTER
TWO

In this city on the banks of a dark river there is a tall nine-story building with four apartments on each floor except the first floor, which was not designed for housing. In an apartment on the story before last, to the left of the elevator, a strange woman, who lives in Zubaida's being, is preparing for the ritual of night travel. Before she goes to bed, she holds her head in both hands, turns it counterclockwise until it is severed from the neck. She then holds it tightly and cautiously like one who carries a heavy glass urn. She puts the head under the tap and cleans the inside with an old brush made especially for washing bottles of curdled milk. She meticulously rubs the inside to rid it of the dreams, lies, and expectations that cling to it. She then puts her hand inside to remove the small renewed hopes that have stuck to the bottom, refusing to emerge, and throws them into the sink. She then pours liquid detergent into the head to rid it of the remnants of great hopes. She turns off the tap and dries the head with recycled paper to protect the environment. She puts the empty, clean head on her neck and turns it clockwise until it settles on her shoulders. She goes back to the living room, stretches out on the sofa, and watches the events racing across her memory, powerless.

The American and British aircraft bombed the port of Umm Qasar in southern Iraq again, after some brave southerners fought back against the British forces that had controlled the port, even as the American army explored the roads and headed for the capital. The sound of artillery increased; she reduced the sound of the television.

For how many years had Zubaida resided in this city? How many closed doors had she lived behind? In this apartment, far from the center of Berlin, which she had moved into in her third year of exile, she could follow car lights through the kitchen window overlooking the dark, quiet street that was mostly engulfed in oppressive silence. The calmness of the long, cold night was interrupted only by the sound of the old tram cars as they tottered along a narrow railroad. It was here that Zubaida had lost the ability to be surprised by things and had begun to dream of warm mornings in cities like Beirut. Rain no longer had a magical effect on her; she could relive its magic in black-and-white movies on screen, seeing it shimmer on the asphalt of cities she imagined as more benevolent. Between the delayed and the postponed, imprudent Time raced as if it were competing with itself, triumphing over the tram cars that disturbed her troubled sleep. She knows that her mood will be different in the upcoming gray morning.

This city had to unite before Zubaida could make her peace with it and smile at its dark colored river and the sea gulls that swim in its freezing waters. She and the city did not know this truth as they first became acquainted. Today, she will rediscover the city once again and accept its invitation to sit by the roadside to chat and to apologize silently to one another. Zubaida had taught this city Arabic and regretted it, for the city came to understand her more than she would have liked.

Surges of foreign armies cross the bridges while an Apache air-craft monitors the roads to Al-Najaf and Babel for them as they march toward Baghdad. Some correspondents remark that Baghdad will be the burial ground of the invaders, while others think that the city will surrender at the approach of the first soldier. This is an inequitable battle and the soldiers, much as they love their country, hate the dictator.

Suddenly, without any warning, a wave of overwhelming fury besets her, as she remembers details of futile conversations that have drained her energy throughout expatriate years. Telling colleagues stories of her country, describing her nostalgia for the palm trees, and the nation's sorrows during the first war with Iran that brought death to her people. Once she had finished talking, indifferent to her longing, they raised their glasses of white wine to resume a Socialist celebration, which typically broke the dullness of the long, stupefying working hours.

The camera roams around, picking up nameless bodies.

In the heavy summer evenings, and before drawing the curtains across her wide bedroom window, Zubaida waits for darkness to fall and makes sure that the long, boring day has ended. Every day, as she remembers walking into the old building housing the international women's organization she worked for when she first came to East Germany, she remembers the vows she has made to leave this emptiness, this void. She hates herself for her reluctance to depart. By now, she has perfected the art of evading these miserable exchanges by silence or by indulging in superficial conversations with the slow-moving, slow-thinking, cleaning women.

A close-up of an invading soldier's face jumps to the screen. . . .

How simple it was to fill the hearts of those two working women with joy during Christmas and New Year celebrations with a bar of soap from the western part of town, a cheap synthetic shawl, or a lipstick.

A soundless explosion on the screen; she turns up the volume a little, hears another explosion, and mutes the sound.

She had felt both sorry and ashamed as she gave those trivial gifts and watched the overwhelming joy in the women's eyes, those women who have, despite their poor education, perfected the game of duality in behavior and thought, a requirement of Socialist society, where long days were consumed by the slogan that everything must serve the proletariat. There will be many more Christmases, and she won't find anyone to bring joy to with trivial gifts.

Tanks fill up the television screen. She presses the remote control to find songs from Baghdad television ("Take the challenge and leave it to the men"). She loves the idea of the sound crowding her memory.

In one of the rooms of the organization she worked for, Helma asked her friend Monica, who had produced a small packet of chewing gum, "Where did you get this gum?"

She gave her a piece and both proceed to chew in a repulsive manner, producing sounds Zubaida could hear and bubbles she saw float out of their mouths. Helma continued, "A gift from your friend in the Yemeni embassy? Doesn't he have a friend that you could introduce me to? A pair of jeans isn't expensive in the diplomatic market, yes? How much is Italian shampoo? I'll give you the money for a bottle in eastern marks if you ask him to buy one for me. I can't take the smell of Socialist shampoo any longer."

Monica, then Helma, looked at Zubaida as she pretended to be reading the *Neues Deutschland* newspaper, pretending to be interested in world news, which she knew only too well that she would not find in this paper. Zubaida left the room and the chatter about jeans and Italian shampoo. She sat in a corner of the cafeteria on the second floor and ordered a cup of coffee, which she did not touch; she wanted only some space for reflection.

Through the window as the glass grows foggy, she saw the snowflakes fall and glimpsed the faraway other half of Berlin. Unlike Helma or Monica, she could cross over there and return whenever she wished. She often crossed over, then came back, always thinking and dreaming of staying there but never doing so. This adventure was no adventure at all, but rather an endeavor without courage. She didn't dare decide to cross over to the western side of the city and never return to a society forever dreaming of freedom. Zubaida realized that her daydreaming was producing tears. Fearful that the waitress in the empty cafeteria would see that her coffee remained untouched, she rose just as the large, generous waitress approached, smiled, and said, "Of course, you don't like Socialist coffee."

When she took the tram that evening, it seemed just like any other time, even to the number of pedestrians on the street. She heard a woman whisper something in her friend's ear about a German who had succeeded in escaping to the other side of Berlin. Somewhat later, she learned that this young man had manufactured a flying balloon, dyed it black, and waited for the wind to blow toward West Berlin. He and his family had boarded in darkness and flown there. The media over the next few days made Communist intelligence in East Berlin seem a shambles, despite the fact that it was an institution that knew the traffic routes of ants in the holes of walls!

Zubaida wondered what this man would have felt during that short journey in the darkness had the East Berlin police shot down the balloon, ending his life at the very same spot he tried to leave it behind.

As Zubaida got off the tram, she noticed a crowd of policemen near the bronze statues of the Socialist military heroes on the hill opposite her apartment. Some policemen were trying to remove the dye that had been hurled nightly at these statues by antiregime activists. She had noticed black stains on the statues when she had left for work in the morning. That evening, she found a note from the local police on her door, asking her to come to the police station. At once, she thought of her permission to stay in East Germany. So she went straight off to the police station where the officer in charge asked her, "No doubt you noticed the dye on the statues of the national heroes?"

"Yes, I saw it in the morning."

"Did you see any persons standing there last night?"

"It would be difficult for me to see anything from my window at night, for it is very dark, and the statues are far away. Besides, I'm not usually curious enough to observe what people do."

"That'll be all. You can go home now. Sorry to bother you at this time."

She was not used to hearing apologies from the police in this part of town, for policemen were known to behave without feeling and, sometimes, without civility. A German citizen might have found this behavior normal, but for her the apology of the German officer felt unsettling.

One day, Abu Rosa arrives from northern Iraq on a visit to Eastern Europe. In East Berlin he visits the few Iraqis who work in the international organization, and in a corner of the cafeteria, on the second floor, begins to narrate his feats in the Communist Party, a customary practice. He boasts, "I took part in a military operation against the Iraqi army. From the mountain, we spotted an armed vehicle that soon was within range of our guns. We hit it with an RPG-7, and then showered it with bullets. No one was spared, except a corporal who emerged from the burning vehicle, walking like an intoxicated person due to the accuracy of the strike. He was bleeding from his shoulder and face, and then he came closer. We didn't want to take him prisoner because he would be a burden, and rules of war forbade us to kill him. He begged us to save him and quench his thirst, but how could we give water to or cure an enemy who may kill our families in Iraq by the dictator's orders? We allowed him to leave, but he didn't know which direction to take. As a result of the shock, he swayed like a drunkard between the rocks."

He begins to laugh as he repeats, "The enemy swayed like a drunkard . . . our strike was so accurate. The comrade who fired the RPG-7 died three weeks later. His name was Abu Karim."

Zubaida listens silently to the speaker and notices that his voice changes as he frowns, stops laughing about the wounded soldier, and begins to seem sad.

"Yes. Abu Karim died in a battle with an Iraqi army unit. We had wanted to conduct a second operation to commemorate the great October Revolution led by Lenin. We arranged everything for this operation, and Abu Karim was not supposed to be one of the team, but when he learned that it was to commemorate the great October Revolution, he insisted on taking part. He was so courageous: He attacked the enemy camp, met Iraqi army fire, and fell as a martyr. We wanted to bury him on top of Pira Makroun Mountain, but enemy fire was very heavy, and so we had to turn back. The following day we explored the area by telescope, but his body was not to be found. They had either burned it, or taken it back to camp to search his pockets. Some may criticize us and say: 'How can you fight your own army? And how can you fight your army while it is fighting its enemies?' Those who say this have to recognize that we are fighting the army of the dictator."

As he speaks, he leans toward Zubaida as if she were the one he was speaking to. Instantly, Zubaida sees her brother on the battlefield with Abu Rosa shooting at him and laughing, while her brother collapses. She runs to the bathroom and throws up the remains of food in her stomach. Others hear her as she coughs. She flushs the toilet, washes her face, and leaves for her apartment without a word.

She gets on a tram and takes a seat. She avoids the eyes of the few passengers. She wants to be alone. Abu Rosa's conversation has confirmed her own views that these creatures of political institutions lead to tomorrow's disasters, a fact that horrifies her. She sees the future as truly bleak. She would like to say: "Your name is not Abu Rosa. You are Abdel Wahed Sharhan from Al-Fouhud County in Nasiriyah, and you chose this name for yourself in honor of Rosa Luxemburg." As if people might hear her thoughts, she turns around to make sure that no one occupies the seats behind her. In the tram, she knows she cannot scream. Lost in reverie, she sees only the heavy fire on all fronts in Iraq. Why did she leave her home in flames? Could she have helped put out the fires? She wakes from her reverie only when the tram stops at the station in front of the hill planted with the statues of the defenders of the Socialist country, the silent memorial that meets her eye each morning and evening.

From her first arrival Zubaida had come to know both parts of the city. She had come when the wall circled its western half and had stayed long after the gray cement stones and barbed wire had gone. The fall of the wall had come as no surprise to her. Much had happened over many years to prepare for this beautiful explosion. She wanted to take part in the celebration, a huge carnival at which history changed before her eyes. Zubaida, who walked slowly on that day, imagined history as an old neighbor leaning against the fence of an old house in the middle of the city, but when she greeted him, he did not hear her. She knew that she was seeing history changing, and she thought to herself that she had better save those memories carefully, for history was happening on her doorstep.

Who could experience such privilege easily? At noon, the city streets were crowded with tens of thousands, stopping traffic, and even metro trains stuck in tunnels. She spent that whole day walking around the city with other people, and when evening came, she felt exhausted. But then she realized that she could not really share all this happiness and joy with the Germans, for the common history that had brought them together had separated her from them. No matter how hard she might try to join them, her joy had to be marginal and resistant to a history she was not part of.

The overwhelmingly joyous expressions of a people she had thought emotionally dead confirmed the borders of her own estrangement and refreshed her sense of her own roots that were still packed up in a suitcase. With the new geographical freedom, other problems would emerge, but she could take a deep breath, and that was really what counted.

She finds herself in a past she alone possesses, and only in it does she sense an old feeling of affinity and an illusory longing that are chained to impossible dreams. The present drops off like a garment she removes from her body whenever she is besieged by the details of alienation from the city's everyday life. She seeks refuge in memory whenever she feels forlorn. How similar this building is to that, this neighborhood to that, and this neighbor to the other. Even the mailbox that she hesitates to open in the entrance of her building is identical to the other small mailboxes. She postpones the opening of letters for hours until she feels calm enough to receive whatever there is to receive, which is often not a source of joy for her today or tomorrow. She opens the mailbox, then carries the letters to her apartment, throws the keys and the letters on the table, and leans on the sofa. She looks at the letters: one from the bank, which she removes without opening, for she knows that it cannot be pleasant; another from the electric company, which she removes as well. She hesitates before a letter from Iraq with a stamp of the dictator's face. Should she open it first? At the back of the envelope, she sees Fouad's name. Is it Fouad, her cousin? She doesn't expect the letter to be from this Fouad and wonders how he got her address. She opens the letter.

"My dear Zubaida, I send you warm greetings from Iraq, and I know this is a surprise. I got your address from your family. I am so sorry that I couldn't write before now, since I am on the front in the war with Iran. I hope you are fine in Europe, far away from this hell. People who live in Europe are, without a doubt, happy and comfortable despite the cold and snow. They are the fortunate ones."

Zubaida smiles as if she were saying: "He has not been introduced to the cities of snow and their inhabitants yet!"

"I wanted to write to you a long time ago, but I have been postponing it. However, today I write, my dear Zubaida, after having been given sick leave from the army. I am not pretending to be sick, I am really unwell, and the doctor has prescribed a certain medication that I could not get. Pharmacies here are bare, except for the empty boxes that cover the shelves. I feel severe pain in my kidneys, and they have given me only painkillers. I need a few boxes of a certain medication. You'll find its name on the back of this page. Your brother was with us at the front. We met once on the front line. He was brave, but he was shooting into the air. Do you understand? I haven't seen him at the front again. Maybe he has been taken prisoner. I hope so— that is better than something else. My wife left me, and our daughter Afaf has grown into a very beautiful young woman. My sister Nariman married my cousin, and her husband is at the front too, and my mother died years ago. I hope this news won't disturb you. We live through such news and receive it casually, for we have gotten used to it. Don't forget to send me the medication. We always remember you with love. Good-bye then."

She folds the letter, puts it in her purse, and rises. The news of her brother at the front and the fact that Fouad had not seen him again hits her hard. She needs a friend to talk to. Her brother has a special place in her consciousness: She had left him when he was a child, and he remains in her memory as a youngster who has not grown up; when she imagines him at the front, she imagines a child carrying a rifle taller than he. Fouad's letter confirms that he shoots into the air, as she has hoped he would, but he has disappeared. "Dear God, let him be taken prisoner," she thinks.

Zubaida weeps, then leaves the apartment in search of Fouad's medication.

She floats over the streets of the city, not feeling her feet treading the ground, as if she were a ghost. Her body feels absent from the city that disappears from her consciousness when she goes to sleep. Asleep, the details of her city of residence leave her memory, and other dust-covered, weary cities emerge. There is no water to quench her patience. All the long years seem empty and useless compared to the years she left hanging behind her. All alien evenings and mornings are rusty stations.

She gets the medication from an Arab doctor she knows, packs it, and hands the package to the post office clerk. She doesn't return home directly but sits in a public park watching the passing faces. A woman with her dog passes by, and she remembers her neighbor Mrs. Schneider and her dog. That woman never returned her greeting, not once. How can people continue to exist among those who keep reminding them that they are strangers?

She feels puzzled and asks herself, Should I tell Ahmed about Fouad's letter and his reference to our brother, whom he had seen only once at the front? Is it all right to bear sad news to those she loves? Maybe they transferred him to another battalion. She lifts the receiver and tries to call her family to see how they are doing, knowing full well that all lines are inoperative. She decides to talk to her brother Ahmed in Tunisia.

She calls and asks him about the family, and he says, "I wrote to them, and they wrote and sent you their regards. They say they're fine."

Zubaida assumes that they did not want to tell him about their brother and news of him at the front. She asks, "What's the latest news from our soldier brother?"

"They didn't mention him in particular, but they said they're all fine, and that, undoubtedly, includes him as well."

She recognizes that his information was inaccurate and that Fouad's letter was more precise.

She says, "Please make sure to ask them about our brother at the front."

He responds, "Do you have news of the family? Have you received a new letter?"

"I received one from Fouad, our cousin. Do you remember him? He asked me for medication because he has renal problems. He wrote, saying that he saw our brother at the front, then never saw him again."

"Maybe he has been transferred to another battalion, who knows. . . ."

"Can you call our family from Tunisia? I have tried but failed."

"I will try, but don't worry. Not to see him at the front is normal. The front is vast, Zubaida. Don't wallow in sorrow before it is time to be sad, please."

She cannot prevent the wild and cruel past from appearing to blend into bloody events on the screen before her. She cannot tear herself away from the remnants of the long, silent time she lived in the eastern part of the city, and felt disdainful toward the servile, depressed faces around her. Zubaida only now understands that the sorrow inside her is not sudden, or accidental, but rather necessary, even essential, to the formation of her consciousness. It is the inexplicable irritability of her rebellious soul, the only thing that gives her pulse continuity. How could she ever have thought that sorrow was marginal to her nature? And how could she not recognize that its light cleanses the soul? She knows now that sorrow will be a significant part of her character, though she continues to seek a way out of abstract misery.

She is now aware of the aggressive and self-confident Western mind, especially if placed beside an Arab mind mired in coma, not functioning. Surrounded by humans outside of the actual essence of existence, she continues to search for critical people who are satisfied neither by native lands nor exiles. She continues to wait. She dreams of absurd floods that drown the dry fields of the soul, then recede and leave the fields green and fecund, suitable for new crops. She makes fun of her naïveté as she recalls the details of illusions and absurd dreams as if some hand has poured cold water over a barren landscape until it disappears. In many autumn mornings that come and go, her soul opens up sometimes like wild spring flowers, and then she forgets the sorrow that sends autumn sunlight through the window and into the apartment. Over the years she has fed on a dream that has become an illusion grown into a reality that she has learned to combat with desperation.

Tomorrow she will begin to rearrange things. She will uncover the disorderly heap of years and draw out a memory— perhaps of a person or an incident she can hold in her hands. As she reaches into the disordered past, she knows that she needs another life to reorganize this chaos.

The air force bombards the road leading to Baghdad International Airport, now a military airport.

War correspondents reveal that huge numbers of soldiers have died in the underground passages between the dictator's palace and the airport, an underground tunnel built by the dictator for circumstances like these. All those who walked through the long tunnel to the airport, to defend it from the American troops, died when the tunnel was bombed. The foreign engineers who had planned this tunnel gave the blueprints to the intelligence agencies of their countries. The whole country is outlined on the invaders' plans, and the dictator is the only idiot.

The war did not begin today, but tens of years ago. It began on the wrong, unprepared-for day when the Iraqi army encircled Al-Rehab Palace to change the regime. Zubaida remembers her grandmother telling her once that, when the soldiers encircled the palace, the young king, Faisal II, came out holding the Koran in his right hand. Her grandmother had talked about how the young king had fallen, covered in his own blood, the blood that stained his white flag. Her grandmother had often said, "Yours is a white flag, Faisal," and she always prayed for him. Her grandmother described the event in details that she had heard or imagined, all grounded in her love for the king. She described the young King Faisal holding the Koran and the white flag and walking toward the soldiers who had attacked Al-Rehab Palace, where the royal family lived. They shot him dead. The king had not yet married. They said he was preparing for marriage, and the people were waiting to celebrate the marriage of the young king. The state employees would get a holiday and a bonus, and some families waited for an official pardon of prisoners that usually accompanied wedding celebrations.

March forward, king, your history has come to an end, and another's history, though still undefined, has arrived. March forward, king, whose smile disappeared in an instant, the instant the first mortar fell on Al-Rehab Palace. March onward, you beautiful king, for the mob will kill you, and the moment of your death shall be a shameful blot on history's page. How grievous to see you as victim. March forward, king, the hooligans will enjoy killing you.

The king advanced toward the soldiers who bombarded the royal palace, while the children cried and the women felt frightened in sight of a monumental event they did not understand. The women then did not realize the meaning of a revolution or a coup d'état, and they didn't know the meaning of an army betraying its king. The army that circled the palace received its orders from its officers in the rear lines. A corporal approached, holding a British gun, in an open car with another machine gun beside him. The corporal examined the shivering, agitated young king and fantasized that he would be the new king sitting on the throne and so aimed his rifle at the king and shot him. He fell, and the blood seeped slowly into his white flag.

She saw it herself: Zubaida at five or six saw the mob running behind a motorcycle, dragging the remnants of a torn body. She did not know yet the meaning of the slogans that the running mob repeated. She did not understand the words, "Long live the nation" and "long live the people." In fact, she cannot remember anything except the crowds in the Adhamiya district running behind this motorcycle, which dragged the remnants of the body tied to it. Her pregnant mother, taken by surprise by the crowd as she stood in Ras Al-Hawash alley on her way to the market, fainted when she saw this blue human heap dragged along the street. One image will stay in Zubaida's mind forever: her grandfather rushing toward her mother, swearing and cursing, as Zubaida stood bewildered, wondering whether the man in a striped gown who disappeared into the crowd with a knife in his hand and the hem of his gown in his mouth was "the people" or "the nation."

The teacher distributed copybooks with a sticker of the emblem of the Iraqi Republic to the first graders. The stickers had been printed with haste to hide the picture of the Iraqi King, Faisal II. Zubaida removed the sticker, which wasn't firmly glued, and the king's picture seemed clearer, and his smile lit up some joy in her soul, an act that drove her classmates, Sarwa and Quais, to do what she had done. The teacher noticed this and was angry. She moved toward them as they stared at the picture of the young, smiling king. They tried to ask why the picture was hidden by the emblem, but the teacher simply shouted at them, and so they tried in vain to reattach the emblem over the king's picture. Afraid that curiosity might infect the other students and drive them to remove the sticker, the furious teacher collected all the notebooks and distributed others with the emblem firmly glued.

That was the first lesson on the first day in National Education: The picture of the smiling king had to disappear from the free copybooks distributed to students at the beginning of the year. Zubaida forgot all about him.

Every morning, Naima, a sixth-grade student, would come to take Zubaida, a second grader, to school with her. She used to sit on the edge of a chair until Zubaida's blind grandmother finished combing Zubaida's long, thick hair, making it into a single braid that, more often than not, did not satisfy her. When the beautiful brunette Naima, whose long, pointed nails were painted in light pink, smiled, Zubaida would be surprised by her white, beautiful, and even teeth, and her own tongue involuntarily moved around her mouth, touched her teeth, measuring the gaps, and frowned.

She cannot now remember anyone of Naima's family except her brother Kamel. In fact, she cannot tell when Naima disappeared from her morning program or when her family moved away.

"Yours is a white flag, Faisal! God bless your soul, grandma," Zubaida says to herself as if she were speaking to her grandmother in the grave, sending her a message from the city of snow, as she imagines King Faisal carrying the Koran and the white flag and approaching the soldiers who had never read elementary-school readers. Then their tanks roamed the streets of Iraqi cities, while others seized the Iraqi broadcasting station, and the second officer of the coup d'état, with little experience in performance, screamed, "All airports and Iraqi borders are to be closed, and officers in charge are to execute these orders."

Women of the royal family did not know where to go. The king's aunt and her child rushed to the Royal Embassy of Saudi Arabia and the prime minister stayed as a guest with friends in the district of Al-Kadhamiya while the huge crowds dragged ministers onto the streets. "The people," the entity which Zubaida had thought was this careless man who carried a knife and bit the hem of his gown, inciting the crowds to kill, reappeared in more than one district, street, and city in Iraq.

Zubaida's grandmother had said that whenever the two rivers went dry; whenever the Tigris and Euphrates overflowed; whenever Iraq was overtaken by pestilence; whenever they dragged people on the street; whenever Iraqis fought one another; whenever life became expensive; whenever the rains were delayed; whenever houses were on fire—it was King Faisal's curse, for they killed him while he came to them in peace and held the holy Koran in his hand.

Her father explained that all had happened because of the absence of consciousness and the spread of backwardness in society. He was sad and lonely. On that day, war began in Iraq: small wars, larger wars, and catastrophic wars between Iraq and its neighbors, and between Iraq and the world.

The name of the officer who ignited the coup d'état and caused the change in Iraq's history appeared. His picture, too, appeared on small stickers that people began to put on the windshields of their cars. Some took refuge in this, intending that their cars would pass without being searched by their fellow citizens, who had volunteered to become the protectors of the First Republic after the police and the secret police had disappeared. The people slept after the first day of chaos and killing. New names appeared and very few asked after the young king who had smiled on the front pages of school notebooks. Zubaida's grandmother no longer said, "Yours is a white flag, Faisal," for it had become stained red. Her memory still held the image of the king who was murdered by wild bullets. The small bullet shot at the young King Faisal grew, multiplied, and transformed itself into shrapnel loaded with banned components that burned the trees and polluted the land and water. Instead of healthy babies, disease grew and spread inside women's wombs.

The country is burning in front of her now, and she doesn't know the extent of the invisible flames. The screen exposes a limited blaze, but she knows that the fire outside the frame of the screen is greater. These are flames beyond Baghdad, extending to her room, kitchen, balcony, and moving on to the world.

In Iraq, Zubaida learned her first lesson in chaos, revenge, and fear, and from her father she also learned bitterness. Her father would rise whenever a woman entered their home or walked into his office at the factory. He would get up, button his blazer, and bow to the woman. His accounts were meticulous; not only in his books but in life. The lessons in killing, revenge, and fear were alien to his consciousness.

"They will not bombard the bridge, they need it, the plan is not watertight," thus comments the political analyst on television when the invading army battalions cross the city of Al-Najaf.

The media inside Iraq sharpens its reportage against the American and British troops. A helicopter goes down, and the pilot is taken prisoner on the road to Al-Najaf. The helicopter was not shot down by antiaircraft missiles that had already disappeared into the palm fields; it fell as a result of technical malfunction. But an old peasant, given an antiquated Bruno rifle, is taught a story in which he is destined to be a hero. He is told: "You shot down the helicopter with this rifle. You must believe that and tell all satellite broadcasting stations how you shot down this helicopter with your old rifle."

You are no hero for this, old man, and you don't even want that, for you have long lived as a hero simply by bearing the hardships of regimes. It has been enough to have lived at the mercy of this life: You are truly a hero for that, old man. The dictator has forced you to become a hero of songs. You used to hate lying and chided your children when they lied. You have values and stories to tell your children and grandchildren, and you are frightened that this falsehood will spread and that you will become the laughingstock of the whole tribe. What if your tribesmen, in their gatherings, told the story of the helicopter that was shot down by a Bruno, and you knew that you were meant by that? How can you drink your bitter coffee with the same relish? Is this not disrespectful of your nobility and kindness? You knew the name of the game, and wished you had died by the rifle they gave you from the museum of antique weapons. You loved folk poetry and hated songs, so they thrust you into songs and pulled you out of real history. You have been tossed into a false history you don't acknowledge. You have seen for yourself the brave men resisting desperately, knowing that they will inevitably die. They resist because they love their homeland and are desperate because they hate the dictator. Sorry, dear old man, for what befell you in the days of war.

This war has not just begun. It has been ongoing since the illiterate corporal shot the young King Faisal. His grandfather was Faisal the First, founder of the modern Iraqi state, the state whose pillars are now falling apart, the descendant of the Hejazi king who tried to unite the offspring of old Iraq: groups of Arabs, Kurds, Turkmen, Assyrians, Mandeans, and other religious and ethnic groups that he succeeded in rearranging into one nation. This nation did not calm down after the king's assassination. How often Zubaida's father told her about the Hejazi king who had united all groups into one nation.

Zubaida recalls getting on the double-decker red bus with her father, for she liked to sit on the second level. Being on the bus with her father pleased her, and from up there, they could see the names of films currently in theaters. She also recalls feeling bored sitting next to him while he played backgammon at a famous café, called "The Parliament." She failed to understand the excitement and commotion of the men as they threw the dice. Her father felt her boredom and told her that other little girls would be coming to the café, but though she watched the door, she would always remain the only little girl there. Her boredom usually ended when they went to a movie theater, where first they entered the manager's room, since her father knew him well and where he always insisted that Zubaida purchase the tickets herself. She would go to the ticket counter, buy two tickets, and her father would expect her to precede him as they entered the theater and climbed the stairs to await the performance. Once they had been late, and the usher had had to use his flashlight, and she had been embarrassed as she walked amid the seats in the dark.

Zubaida had found freedom in the darkness of the theater, a darkness that had kept her apart from the "other" since her childhood, a darkness that could still transport her into a magic dream on the screen and into other worlds. She could bathe in the seas and oceans of the screen and soar into skies, sniffing flowers in gardens, exploring houses with velvet curtains, feeling love, and glowing with music. She felt secure and happy because her father was sitting by her, and he respected her freedom and her passion for the movies.

Gone are those simple days of enjoying film. Now as she watches live documentation on film, she cannot feel the same passion. Just as she lost her father, she has lost her youthful sense of pleasure.

The rhythm of war heightens on television.

Her grandmother sat near the cupboard and told her sad stories that could break hearts. Zubaida could not imagine the
first house without the old cupboard standing in the corner of
the room, the heavy cupboard that was never moved. No one
dared use it because her grandmother always said that it had
been entrusted to her, and that its owners would come one day
to retrieve it. Zubaida tried to imagine the Jewish woman who
had offered the cupboard to her grandmother for a very cheap
price in the days of looting in the forties, when Iraqi Jews were
forced to emigrate. When her grandmother told her this story,
Zubaida never understood why she had refused to buy her
Jewish neighbor's cupboard, or why it was kept here, if she
hadn't bought it? When she asked, her grandmother always
said: "It is not right to buy something from someone in need,
someone whose soul is attached to a thing. This would be
a sin."

Her grandmother's solution had been to give the Jewish
woman the money she needed, and to promise to keep the cupboard until she returned. But she had never returned, and now
her grandmother had gone as well. No one remained, and
Zubaida no longer remembered what had become of the piece
of furniture. Yet its image remained in her memory, like a distant dream. Just before this piece had vanished, suddenly, a
small crack had appeared in its crystal mirror.

When Zubaida had asked about the meaning of the word
"looting," her grandmother said, "When the Jews immigrated to
Palestine, they left their houses here. They took their gold and
money, but left the heavy things behind, and so people rushed
to their houses and took furniture, electric fans, cookers, and
fabric from shops. 'Looting' means to take something that

doesn't belong to one without paying for it. This is a sacrilegious act that God Almighty will not accept and will punish for, when the Day of Judgment comes."

In those days, very few people had heard of a man named Adas, but one morning they heard newspaper vendors yelling on the streets, "Today is Adas's hanging." His name appeared on the front pages of the morning papers. Adas was a Jewish tradesman who owned a shipping company and several ships that transported food supplies among the Gulf, India, and Iraq. He had built a scarlet castle in Al-Basrah that resembled a ship with poles that looked like sail masts, which later were said to be means of transmitting information to Jewish organizations. The royal government decided to hang Adas, the Jewish tradesman of Basrah, so as to frighten other Jews who worked as fabric retailers in Baghdad. Their warehouses were full of brightly colored fabrics from India and other places. No one had ever excelled in this trade like the Jews. When the Jews were made to leave their homes and warehouses in Iraq, people were seen carrying fabrics folded over wooden cylinders, cloth ends trailing behind them as they transferred them hastily into carts near the warehouses, pushing as they ran to their houses to store the beautifully colored fabrics. Others looted chairs, wooden tables, paintings, and food, while the helpless Iraqi police were busy protecting the Jews and moving them to camps in preparation for their move to Palestine.

A man on one of Baghdad's plazas stood, passionately delivering a speech and shouting at the top of his voice: "Is it possible for Zion to be given an eternally holy land? By what law can Zion be given such an eternally holy land?"

The speaker charged that Arab treason had led to the selling of the Palestinian homeland. Amid the speaker's shouting and the transferring of Jews into trucks, the police at times lashed the backs of those carrying stolen fabrics, and, at times, beat the crowds around the orator, incriminating the forfeiture of land and honor. Zubaida's grandmother alone paid for the wooden cupboard. She never opened it to see whether it was empty, and considered it a charge until its owners returned.

After almost half a century, and with the sounds of artillery and the images of war, the media announces the return of some Iraqi Jews to visit the graves of their families. Amid the fires and destruction of war, the Jewish woman's cupboard jumps into Zubaida's vision. She imagines that she is seeing it on the television screen and that it has been transformed into a gigantic cupboard with one strangely decorated door that Zubaida does not remember. Its crystal mirror now has a fissure from top to bottom. The cupboard grows larger and larger, holding within it the image of the entire burning city.

On clear days, Zubaida used to walk beside her father and sometimes run ahead when he took her to the factory where he worked. When he got to his office, he would open the ledgers to register numbers whose meaning she couldn't comprehend. These were long ledgers that he needed both hands to open. He would open the leather covers of them, then turn the pages, take out his elegant Parker pen, and write. Usually, he would hang up his Sidare, a Faisal style cap, on a hook, but sometimes, when he was late, it would remain on his head as he wrote the numbers, and then, suddenly, he would realize that he had forgotten to hang it up. Eidan the Mandean would bring him a small glass of tea, and, for Zubaida, a bottle of lemonade. Her father would ask Eidan, "Have you set a date for your wedding? Remember, I promised Zubaida she could attend and see the marriage rituals of the Mandeans."

Zubaida stood next to her father on the bank of a river near the palm fields far from the city. At the edge of the river, the priest, a few white hairs in his black beard, raised his hands in prayer. She did not understand the meaning of the words, nor did she comprehend their profundity that day; she saw only their effect on all those present and only later on did she understand the meaning of this chant:

In the name of the eternally alive
I came by His supreme power, and my will.
Water that gives me power, constantly, leads me to baptism;
To accept purification wearing the garment of light and putting
    on my head
A wreath of flowers
My given name has been bestowed upon me.

The priest, in his white religious garb, stepped into the river. Behind him Eidan stepped with his bride. Zubaida had wanted to get closer to the river, but was anxious about not falling in the mud and spoiling the shoes and dress that her father had bought for this occasion. Zubaida had stood bewildered as she watched the priest, Eidan, and his wife in the river in their wet clothes. The priest took hold of Eidan's head and immersed it in the water three times. Zubaida was frightened lest the man should drown and die, and so held on to the edge of the jacket of her father, who was trying to explain the beauty of the ritual, saying that Eidan, whose head was submerged in the water by the priest, was in fact being cleansed and purified by the water. After Eidan had submerged his head three times, the priest gave him a piece of bread and put his hand on Eidan's head, murmuring the words of baptism, and then made him drink a sip of river water. He then repeated the same ritual with the bride: holding her hair, submerging her in the river three times, then giving her a piece of bread and a sip of river water. Everyone came out of the water, Eidan's eyes met Zubaida's, and he smiled at her, and she felt relieved that he was all right.

The guests moved into a clearing. Four pillars held a roof

made of palm reeds. The sun's rays fell through the roof and danced on the leaves covering the ground. A breeze moved among the trees. The bride, groom, and priest disappeared and then returned in their wedding clothes. Zubaida felt overwhelmed by the bewitching, strange atmosphere that she had never felt in weddings of the Adhamiya district. Two young boys entered, each carrying a plate with a ring on it, one with a red stone and another with a green stone. These were the same rings that Eidan had bought the day he had taken her with him to Zahrun the jeweler, the day she had been fascinated by the gold and by the minute palm trees and camel convoys engraved in silver; by the tiny silver ships colored in blue enamel, and by the decorated picture frames, one of which had had the king's picture inside and the royal crown on top. She had no idea how much Eidan had paid Zahrun the jeweler, but she believed he had paid a lot of money, and she had said as much to her father when she went back to his office. Now she understood why Eidan had bought the rings. The priest was now putting the green ring on Eidan's finger and the red on the bride's. With other guests, Zubaida moved forward toward the wedding buffet, which abounded in bread, grilled fish, dried fruit, raisins, walnuts, almonds, and salt. She took a piece of bread, put some fish on it, and ate her fill. She then helped herself to raisins and almonds. As she watched people sprinkling roses, sugar, and almonds over the newlyweds, her father said, "They are thus wishing them good health and a sweet, blessed life."

As she watches the images of war on television, she sees that the planes bombing Baghdad are burning this beautiful day as well.

In 1963, the officer who had begun the coup d'état of 1958, who knew the homeland and loved it, and who did not know the game of politics, was brought in chains along with others by young boys proud of their green uniforms and the two letter badges on their arms. They dragged a man who had made history and forcefully pulled him out of it. They executed him. A national guardsman had asked him three, maybe four questions, and then he was shot; his shirt, as he had wanted it to be, was drenched in blood. The man was not a traitor, but he had engaged in a difficult battle alone. When the people had gathered like sea waves, he had spoken to them, saying: "I will leave this world without possessions; only with this shirt, which will be soaked in blood."

Not one of the human waves had supported the man. Only a few hundred poor people, for whom he had built houses befitting their humanity, in a land rich in oil, knew him at all. They knew the story of his negotiations with the British delegation. When the British came to negotiate with him about Iraqi oil, he took them to the poor belt that surrounds Baghdad, the capital of Harun Al-Rashid, surrounded by thousands of huts built on the edge of stagnant waters, behind an earthen fence known as Al-Sadda, the dam. The gallant officer stood with the British delegation to show them a miserable world where children went barefoot. The negotiators produced their silk handkerchiefs and put them over their noses to disguise the odors. The officer turned to them and said, "I brought you here to negotiate on behalf of these people." That day, in that poverty-stricken spot, the British recognized that this officer would be a problem. At that moment, they made the decision to get rid of him. Then, when they came back to negotiate further, he insisted on speaking his own language although he was competent in theirs, a second sign emphasizing that he would be difficult to deal with.

The officer died at the Iraqi broadcasting station. This was the third time he had been to those rooms. The first time, a few days after the coup d'état, he had congratulated the employees there. The second time, when the opposing powers were beginning to sabotage the country in preparation for an uprising, he had gone to the radio station himself, gathered the directors and writers, and had begun to narrate the plot of a radio drama which he called "The Price of Treason," and which was written, produced, and broadcast on the same day. The drama portrayed young men who were given specific sabotage tasks to betray their homeland. The officer, Abdel Karim Qassem, instructed the director: "Render the dialogue among the traitors in a horse-driven coach. Do not let them meet in a cellar or a house. Let them meet in a coach moving through the streets of Baghdad, and let us hear them speak in whispers about their tasks as we hear the horse's hoofs moving. Make the coachman an accomplice."

The third time he was executed in the radio station.

The sound of an explosion on television. . . .

Zubaida sees men on the screen. She doesn't know whether they are soldiers or officers, for they have taken off their shirts, waving them, surrendering to whoever happens to see them. In defeat, all military ranks are equal. The dictator, with all his medals, the corporal, and the soldier who has no medals, all are equal. The dictator was not a military man, and all his medals were fake. They were nothing but decorations made for him by the tailor and certainly not by victories, for he had won no victories except over his own people. Now there are none to give orders and none to receive them; there is only a mass of defeated men. Zubaida oscillates between gloating over and weeping about the fall of the homeland, knowing that the doors that had been locked are now chained.

The dictator will fall in a few days, his guards will surrender, and the foreign soldiers will open all of the doors.

Abdel Karim Qassem, why did all that happen to us? Why did

you suffer and dream only to end up alone in the radio station, lost and waiting for a drifting nonentity to shoot you and your dreams? Is this not a replay of the corporal who shot the king? Did you not recognize the rules of the game, benevolent man? You sat alone, your words undocumented, in a closed room with an announcer watching you through a glass window, no one hearing what you told your murderers before they shot you. History has not documented your words, leader, but why did all that happen?

In 1963, the leaders of the Iraqi Communist Party revealed the location of their first secretary, Salam Adil. Some members of those they call the National Guard found him and at first blindfolded him. Their leader, Al-Saady, had instructed: "Don't kill him, I want him alive, but I want him completely weakened so that his party will also be weakened." The bases of the party fell apart, but the leader remained steadfast until they plucked out his eyes. Then he died.

Later, one of those who had given testimony against Salam Adil said, "When I was in Qasr Al-Nihaya, the royal palace now turned into headquarters for the torture of prisoners, where we were taken after the coup d'état, they brought in Salam Adil, blindfolded and in shackles, and threw him down next to me. I greeted him, he recognized my voice, and told me that he was now in Qasr Al-Nihaya, and explained how they had taken him from home, passed through the Liberation Square, Al-Tahrir, crossed the Republic Bridge, Al-Jumhuriyah, until they reached Al-Khir Bridge, then turned right and entered Qasr Al-Nihaya where they dumped him. Salam Adil could see Baghdad and knew its bridges, alleys, and prisons, even blindfolded."

Then the detention centers, prisons, and police stations were filled with people. "Those who are not with us are against us," repeated the insurgents who had taken power in February 1963, and now said the American president, Bush, the son, in this ongoing war in front of Zubaida's eyes.

The doors of sports arenas were thrown open to accommodate the prisoners. Movie theaters closed down, and stars no longer appeared on the screens. The poor continued to compose tales of Abdel Karim Qassem, who had become president of the first republic of Iraq on July 14, 1958. They called him "the leader," and he had built a large city to replace the shacks. Those poor people could now look at the moon when it was full and visualize an image of "the leader." They stood in groups pointing at the moon and saying, "Look, we see the image of 'the leader' on the surface of the moon." The story spread all around Iraq until the phenomenon of gathering and staring at the moon became a tradition in the country for many years to come, especially on the roofs of poor people's houses.

The poor gathered at night on rooftops in what seemed to be a secret society. The Shiite religious man, Sayed Alaa, moved stealthily through alleys, going up to the rooftops, walking through every house, talking calmly but theatrically, as he stared toward the sky, constructing from its dark rocky surface two eyes, a nose, a mouth, and a military cap like the one "the leader" used to wear. He would outline his moustache, and the poor would reconstruct the image of "the leader" in their imaginations and fix the image to the shadows of the moon's rocks.

Some let fly a rumor that "the leader" had not died and that he would come back one day when they would ask his forgiveness for what had happened to him. They believed that the dead man's body with a soldier spitting on it was simply a military man's body killed during the coup d'état, its face made to resemble "the leader" who was still alive, moving across Iraq, rallying his followers to reseize power.

Hajj Abdullah was one of those who believed this theory. He believed that the men of the new regime had brought in a dead soldier who resembled "the leader," had made up his face, and had shown him to the people on television as the dead leader. To convince the people that "the leader" was still alive, he offered to tell the National Guards that "the leader" was hiding in Husseiniyat Al-Zahraa mosque. Let's see how they will act, he said. If they laugh at me, make fun of me, and call me crazy, this will mean that they have really killed "the leader," and if they raid Al-Husseiniya to search it, this will mean that he is still alive. The people were watching from Sayed Alaa's window when Hajj Abdullah went toward the National Guard headquarters to tell them that he had seen a man who looked very much like "the leader" going through Husseiniyat Al-Zahraa. Quickly, communication began through wireless sets, and military cars arrived and circled Husseiniyat Al-Zahraa. Then the National Guard soldiers appeared and looked for Hajj Abdullah but could not find him. That day, people decided that "the leader" was still alive. His image disappeared from the face of the moon and became a shadow on the rocks scattered on the distant silver sphere.

People were still further convinced that "the leader" was alive when an Iraqi radio station in Bulgaria broadcast part of an old speech of his, which they thought was a new one directed to the Iraqi people. The people thanked God that "the leader" had reached one of the Communist countries, where he had been given asylum, and still thanked God that one day he would come back to free Iraq.

Iraq's tragedy lies in its politics. Her father always used to say this. He knew only too well that Iraqi political institutions lacked clarity of vision and unconditional love for the homeland. When he talked to his friends as he played backgammon at The Parliament Café the young Zubaida would look at her father's friends as they listened to him: She would see him as the teacher with his pupils. It was not easy to talk profoundly in cafés then, and once, when her father had held forth, she had heard someone tell him, "The wall has ears, Abu Ahmed." That day, her father did not comment on the warning against speaking so analytically, but rather objected to his being addressed as Abu Ahmed. He used to say, whenever they addressed him thus, "I am Abu Zubaida, the father of Zubaida, for she is my eldest child," and the men would be astonished and look at one another in disbelief.

Nights had become silent in those days, and her father no longer went to Abu Nawas Street on the bank of the river Tigris with the family to eat grilled fish over an open fire. When she asked him why, he would tell her, "The fish have traveled to Al-Basrah," and she would try to believe this story.

It took only nine months to split the new government and transfer the discord into a battle between two diverse factions within that very same organization. A struggle ensued between the military and the National Guard in which the military finally took over the National Guard, who had filled up the sports fields, prisons, and movie theaters with detainees. People left the prisons and detention camps psychologically and physically maimed. The urge to leave grew inside Zubaida, especially after she had lost the most important reason to stay: her father. He had represented the meaning of civilization and the meaning of freedom. Her father had been at odds with his reality and at odds with his homeland.

CHAPTER
THREE

Estrangement has colored shadows, all derivatives of black. Sunday, in summer and winter, is one of those darkly clad shadows. On summer Sunday evenings, she sits on her unadorned balcony, plunging into memories of a future that will not come. Hers is the only balcony in the building without potted flowers or decorative plants. Forlorn and abandoned, even the sun shines more wanly on it. The balcony seems an autonomous world. At times, except for a few sand dunes, it appears to be an empty desert. At other times, it transforms itself suddenly into a polar space covered with snow that doesn't melt. A satellite dish dwells on the balcony, a huge, frightening metal ghost that captures the world passing through its wires, which endure the fiercely cold winds of the long winters. This seemingly stupid metal object is dangerous and daunting, a silent bulk that contains the boisterous and oblivious world.

Each time Zubaida goes out on the balcony to drink her coffee, she faces this mysterious iron bulk. She feels apprehensive as she glances at the three black eyes fixed inside the concave dish of this dumb, cold form. In summer, as the delayed darkness descends, she rushes into her small living room to celebrate the end of another day. Relief temporarily seeps into her body.

The city has two faces; the wall has disappeared, but two faces remain. The city is a twin—two women—both living in Zubaida's consciousness. On autumn mornings, the first woman wakes up in a bad mood; frowning, she walks down the long, dark hallway and into the bathroom at the end of the apartment. She leaves the bathroom, changes her clothes, and departs for her dreaded job, wishing that another long, heavy day would end before it even begins. On another day, the other woman wakes to an overwhelming delight in life and its rowdiness. Before she heads for the small bathroom, she listens to joyous music. Then she sits on her spacious balcony, in her new apartment in the throbbing heart of the city, drinking light-colored Arabic coffee perfumed with cardamom and talking to the neighbors' cat that has crossed over to her balcony to greet her. At night, the first woman remains depressed, thinking of escaping her dark day by sleeping deeply. She takes a hot shower, swallows a sleeping pill, and runs into the past to travel through its dreams. The second woman returns from work exhausted yet exhilarated. She rests for a while, then takes a refreshing, cold shower, and decides to spend the evening under the starlight.

Zubaida digs her nails into the layers of difficult times and sketches the threads of the sun over the walls of the strange city. She retrieves light from the pores of her memory and scatters it in bundles on the roads ahead of her as she walks in search of some function for her pale day. She continues to fill her spirit with a hope that vanishes as she glimpses it. She feels no warmth. She travels on city trains, ascends the stairs, gets off at another station and sits with Time, which passes by quickly, riding the old yellow cars, keeping the unemployed, like herself, company, and reading, with great boredom, the colored morning papers. When she gets to her destination and leaves the train, Time still remains seated, lifts its eyes from the paper and, with a sardonic smile on its lips, waves good-bye to her.

Today, she does not stop at the lottery salesman, but rather sits in a corner of a café, sipping a cup of tea. She toasts the day that has gone and feels content waiting for another illusion to arrive with evening. In front of her stands a man selling newspapers—a nice young man who could have been a singer, a writer, or even a train engineer. She imagines herself, now that she is practically unemployed, standing in his place, and he in hers. She imagines many people changing places: a president and a beggar; a prostitute and the head of a women's union; a murderer and a supreme judge; and a garbage collector and a bank manager. Is it not a matter of chance and contacts? She has been facing the street to watch the passersby, but now she wants to look at the people in the café and think about the differences between them and her. So she moves to another seat to face them. They are laughing as they sip tea and coffee. They are in harmony. Perhaps they had met in discord, but then they had fought and reconciled their differences in a second, while she is unable even to make peace with herself. She asks herself, Why am I so alone? Why is friendship so rare for me? She feels her failures accumulating so that she can only hide in a corner where she is incapable of having company!

She returns to her first seat and continues to watch the street, holding on to her own world, to the past that refuses to abandon her. The details of a disturbing dream emerge as she stares at the strangers walking by. In the dream, her face is fixed on a man's shadow, the details of which she cannot make out because a dark fog drifts from her head and obscures his identity. If she is lucky, in that recurring dream, she will get a glimpse of his face as the dark fog vanishes. He too moves off, out of her vision, and so she dreams on. When the dream ends, the gray boredom sets in and stays. Illusion lures her into thinking the dream is real, and so she continues to wait for life to begin. She doesn't understand herself. She imagines that she accidentally stood in the path of a storm, then bad luck came to stay with her.

This man has died for some reason that has to do with her nature, or at least that is how she tries to understand her feelings of great loss. And since she knows she never pulled the trigger, she blames bad luck or unknown others. At such times, she feels dizzy and wants to escape her own body.

The waiter sets a plate with the bill before her, as if waking her from sleep. He stands before her indifferently, reminding her of the triviality of a day that will also pass. She pays him and walks alone through the city streets. At the bus stop, she bumps into Sumaya, an Iraqi woman who worked with her for many years in the international women's organization, a stone citadel that she regards as a prison, guarded by blond statues devoid of human features. The encounter with Sumaya is simple and warm, tinted faintly by sorrow and an old reproach that is no longer valid. She sees Sumaya as a strange product of illusions for which she has paid willingly. Content with life, Sumaya cannot escape illusion, nor can she revise her convictions. She has chosen the easy way forward, and like many others, has buried or hidden parts of herself. Zubaida feels sad that the conversation with this kind woman cannot be extended and remain truthful. On her way back, she walks streets crowded with people hurrying as if they had all just left the same huge workplace and were speeding toward many houses dispersed around the city. She sees cafés full of life and light, and she feels the cool evening breeze blowing an early spring warmth. In the quiet apartment, she asks herself, Is this all?

She doesn't remember when she arrived or that she lay down on the old leather sofa in the living room or that she turned on the television. Now she reduces the sound of the television and leaves the light on as the announcer speaks without a voice. Then she drags herself on cold feet to her small bedroom, where she throws herself on the black metal bed, which reminds her of her grandmother's bed and which seems like a corpse lying beside the cold white wall. The lighted computer screen on the desk opposite the bed summons her to write, and so she rises abruptly, as if she has been bitten by something. She sits before the computer as if she were waiting for an unknown and unscheduled train to peel into a station and offer her salvation. Then she gets tired of staring at the white light of the screen, and when she cannot write a single line, she convinces herself that she is suffering from a headache that can only be cured by a cup of heavy black tea and a substantial news broadcast. She turns off the screen, drags herself to the kitchen, and makes a pot of tea, putting it on a tray with a cup and a sugar bowl. She sits on the sofa in the living room and gives life back to the announcer who inhabits the television. She pours the tea but doesn't drink it.

Insomnia comes at its scheduled time exactly; it comes to add anxiety to her already troubled sleep. It does not knock at the door, but rather enters without permission and sits on the edge of her bed, gently putting its hand on her shoulder. She opens her eyes in the direction of the cold, white wall and lies still. She gets up with routine difficulty after a few seconds, making it a point to ignore Insomnia as it sits there curiously watching her. On such endless nights, Memory delights in choosing persons who have been sleeping for long in its corners and amuses itself by removing the dust of time from them and putting them in front of Zubaida's eyes.

That is Laila, the young blond student standing there, smiling a big smile that often hid embarrassment or some other repressed emotion. She presses her schoolbooks to her chest as she walks to school. She has come from the north to live with her sister Seham, her brother Mahmoud, her father, and her elderly aunt, who knows no Arabic except greetings and a few other words placed into awkward sentences. In the evenings of a summer long ago, Zubaida used to visit her best friend Laila. After stifling morning hours and energetic household chores late in the afternoon as the sun began to go down, she would prepare for a visit to Laila. She would take a cold shower, comb her long hair as if she were getting ready for a special event, then leave the house and cross the two streets that separated her house from Laila's. Laila and her family boarded in two rooms of a large house shared with others, but Zubaida entered only one room, for Laila's aunt always sat in the other. Laila left school to marry a young man she loved and soon gave birth to a girl she called Farida.

In the darkness of this night, Laila's beautiful white teeth glitter as she returns, youthful, from the past, her shadow merging with the shadow of her sister Seham, as if Time has forgotten her standing at Zubaida's doorstep, weeping and unable to enter. Even now, Seham continues to lament the loss Zubaida suffered, although Zubaida never once revealed to her the secret of her love. Yet Seham knew without words and came to cry with her over her aborted dream; she came to mourn with her through invisible tears while Zubaida remained bemused, not knowing what to say. Laila sits quietly on the edge of a chair in the dark living room turning the pages of her school copybooks with utter boredom, while Mahmoud sits smoking a cigarette and smiling shyly, and Seham covers her pale, thin, white face with her black abaya, hiding tears she has held back since she first wept for Zubaida's early loss, when Zubaida hadn't expressed the agony of that sad evening. Zubaida sits on the sofa and watches Laila as she gets up and walks toward the balcony, opens the shutters, and disappears inside them. As if preparing to get up, Mahmoud wraps a cigarette stub in a small piece of paper, puts it in his trouser pocket but, before rising, suddenly evaporates. Seham, who never stops weeping silently, wipes her tears with the hem of her abaya, stands up, walks to the corridor, enters the large mirror hanging on the wall, and vanishes. Zubaida feels stifled, she opens all the windows of her apartment, letting the cold breeze in; she leaves the windows open to allow the shadows of her past to depart, goes back to her bed, and dozes off.

In the morning she extends her hand angrily toward a heap of photographs; a pile that increases and decreases as it chooses.

She extracts a handful. She cannot identify either the child looking into a pale void of space in front of him or a girl who resembles herself. Her amnesia angers her, and she throws the photographs into the sunlight, and they disappear instantly. On a clear summer evening she recharges her memory as she discovers the two silver horns of the newborn crescent in an alien sky. She looks to the crescent she is familiar with and asks it to spread light over a forgetfulness that she fears, a forgetfulness that is creeping toward her. She calls for its help; for it is the same crescent that turns, every time, into a full, round moon then dissolves in an eternal ceremony. It is and it will always be that which spreads its cold, silver light upon her forgotten bed on the roof of a small house in summer evenings as she listens through the small transistor to songs selected by others, and sleeps accompanied by a very mundane dream. This bed is still there, under the scorching sun, on the rooftop of the house she abandoned the day the mundane dreams became impossible, unattainable hopes. Once she had been certain that she could, whenever she pleased, restore the past sequentially, exactly as in film, from the beginning up to the point known as the present. But now she knows how difficult it is to find the strong, invisible thread tying the tail of the past with what is still to come. Holding a colorless past in one hand and a pale, artificially colored present in the other, she must rearrange boxes covered with thick dust.

Summer escapes and returns, the year ends and returns again, dragging its days to her balcony once more. Bitten by a freezing breeze that has crept into her bed from a window that she has left open, she wakes at dawn and cannot go back to sleep. On winter days she is not tempted by a pale sun to leave the apartment. Despite the years, she has never grown used to the snowy winter or its fearful nights, but she continues to hang her dreams on the walls at which she once hated to look. The walls are dreary, alien, lifeless, but she has gradually grown used to them. Although Zubaida has waited and hoped for something to happen, something to shatter the boredom of the days and nights, deep inside she remains terrified of skidding dangerously on hope.

Her neighbor closes the door of his apartment, and thus she knows the time is nine-thirty. People here live and walk according to the hands of clocks. She wonders whether he hears her through the walls. Across the long nights, in her bedroom, she sculpts time into small statues she places on the wide windowsill. He had once told her, when she met him walking his dog in his nightly routine around the dark building—elated probably as a result of drinking—that he sometimes eavesdrops to hear the songs she listens to. He even confessed, reluctantly, that he had enjoyed listening to those strange songs. She had looked away and said to herself, "You are at my mercy now." She wanted to tell him that she does not like the songs he heard, that she likes Wagner and the gold of the Rhine and that the Flying Dutchman's ship sails through her head in search of salvation. But she said only that she was happy to hear that.

There is something inside the soul that no one can reach, and only there can freedom reside. The doorbell of the adjacent apartment rings; no one rings her doorbell, she misses nothing here, even the places she has become used to over the years remain without memory. She dreams of being on the shore of a distant, blue ocean, on a red boat with sails resembling the wings of a butterfly the color of warm milk. She dreams of sailing to seek Time and never returning. Zubaida knows she is being obstinate when she says to those who ask her about her expatriation that she has become accustomed to a certain pattern of life, but she knows that this oversimplifies her pain. She has paid an undeservedly heavy price for her mistakes, despite their gravity.

Her feelings of alienation harden and become as sharp as a knife, then soften again; she kneads them and makes a new prison for herself, even as she pours cold water on her dreams and imagines dissolving them all later on.

On spring evenings, before she returns to her desolate apartment, she bathes in the rain, stealthily evading the eyes of the city, and turning around to meet the eyes of the dreamy girl she once was. She wishes she could sit with her to talk and to caress her hair, but she cannot; for there is nothing left of this girl except this woman. She enters her dreary apartment, and before she takes off her old coat, she stands in front of the large mirror in the corridor and speaks to herself, complaining about the harshness of the country that has betrayed her passion for life, and the depressing place she lives in, and how she hopes that the blue ocean is as bright as she imagines it. She hides from the emptiness that follows her, and as soon as it disappears or forgets her, she begins planning. She begins in the middle of a road she walks again and again, in the hope of arriving, though she knows that the road is circular and closed to her. Yet she continues to search for an opening to the sun, to the end of the road. She remains distant from the light of many suns, which rise from diverse directions simultaneously. She has silently withdrawn to the darkness of thick shadows, which drown her and all that surrounds her until she no longer sees her way and is lost. Only her unwavering conviction that there is light outside the border of her vision alone consoles her through the endless waiting.

Gray envelops Berlin, spreading gloom over pavements, the faces of people, and trees. The absence of color mixes morning and evening hours, and thus, Zubaida cannot tell the time. Perhaps this is the secret of the intimate relationship that has developed between her and her wristwatch since the day she arrived here; she resorts to the watch whenever she feels lost between morning and evening. She continues to live, clinging to a powerful stimulant, which accompanies her as with quick steps she enters a small café, looking for the familiar. When she finds an empty, secluded place, she hurries to it and sits staring at the wall before her. She gets up and removes her old black leather coat and unwraps the heavy woolen shawl from her neck. In an affected self-confidence, she hangs the coat and shawl on a nearby hook, then sits again. She relishes this self-confidence and stands up again, reaches for her coat and shawl and places them on the empty chair beside her. She imitates others' indifference. She removes her eyeglasses, puts them into a leather purse, and leaves it on the table before her. She stares stupidly even as she begins to feel oppressed by the overheated room. Discreetly, she wipes away the sweat beads that have collected on her frowning forehead and discovers that she cannot identify faces without her glasses and so puts them over her nose. The waiter, who looks like an army general, ignores her, and so when she signals him to come, she imagines that he looks at her punitively. He asks her what she wants in a tone of politeness mixed with clear animosity. She stammers as if she were frightened by her daring and his question. The "general" brings her a cup of coffee, which she drinks reluctantly, for she doesn't like coffee and knows neither why she has asked for it nor whether she has. But she doesn't object and resorts quickly to escaping, the best option of the defeated. On the street, she searches for familiarity among things—among the pavement stones, and among the birds swimming in the river near her apartment. She seeks the companionship of the dispersed light on the walls of houses but doesn't find it.

Berlin awakens to a snowstorm, and Zubaida hides in the artificial warmth coming from the distant, centrally heated railroad station. When the cold arrives, it stays for days, but she finds the artificial heating heavy and tiring. The coldness then disappears and is replaced by a vacuum, then comes giddiness, perhaps due to the many long trains that enter the station, which are also too warm. The excessive warmth bothers her, and she feels hampered by a heavy winter coat, a burden under which her small body suffers. She climbs the stairs to platform number seven with contrived energy and when she gets there, she stops for a moment to catch her breath and welcome a cold breeze that restores the sensation of her own body. She approaches the platform and squeezes herself between those waiting for the arriving trains. Fast trains pass by without stopping and others enter the station, stop briefly, then depart. She doesn't know how much time remains before her fast train will arrive. She searches for a place to sit, but finds none until someone leaves, when she rushes to the cold wooden bench and breathes in relief. She produces a small book from her purse, opens it, and tries to read. The letters dance over the lines at first, then slip over the space of the glossy white paper, leaping eventually to the platform, and running to hide in the empty Coca-Cola cans scattered here and there. Some letters climb onto the heads and shoulders of passengers; others squeeze between the small bags and luggage. Zubaida observes the small black creatures without surprise, as they make fun of her, cackling away and filling the platform with a hubbub that no one hears. She is used to this game. For years now, Zubaida has thought that this is their revenge against her, for these crooked, twisted shapes have experienced her lack of seriousness and her inability to concentrate. Perhaps they have realized that Zubaida has been captivated by a fever to travel, that the idea of departure has enveloped her being and crippled her. Still, it is a fever that has transformed her into a creature who resembles a suitcase ready to be shipped inside a train or on a ship for a distant destination. In reality, she has not left this city for ages and feels incapable of deciphering the secret of her phenomenal patience.

A clear, sonorous voice announces the arrival of train number 632 coming from Florence that will stop briefly then continue its trip north. The trip north reminds her of a distant past when her school had arranged a trip to Khankin in the north of Iraq, and she could not get her parents' approval to go, and so her classmates took the bus, and she stayed at home. That was the beginning of her journey through the circle of silence. Imprisonment always begins in childhood and so does the dream of freedom. Her parents had told her that the place was far away, that the road was dangerous, and that she had all her life to visit Khankin and other cities of the north and south. But life has passed, and she has seen none of those cities. She is still sitting in the railway station without a filled suitcase, without moving. A train arrives from Paris and another leaves for Vienna. The world is small and trivial, yet Khankin is still distant. Time goes by monotonously, with a boring, repetitive tempo parallel to the movement of the vehicles, and the fugitive letters return to the lines of the book in her purse. She no longer hears the sonorous voice on the microphones. Trains come and go, and the pavement fills with travelers, people seeing others off, and people welcoming arrivals. The space empties, and then fills up again. The motion of the trains makes her feel a strange dizziness as her eyes stare into emptiness. She puts her hand into her coat pocket and feels a ticket and her passport. With the other hand she feels her suitcase as if she were making sure that everything were in place. There she remains seated like a lifeless statue. An hour or two passes. Zubaida stands up and, without any hesitation, puts her hand inside her pocket, takes out the ticket and tears it up, throwing the shreds on the pavement. She carries the empty suitcase out of the station to return to the city that she knows.

CHAPTER
FOUR

On television, officers and soldiers run unarmed in Baghdad.

Is it possible that his old friends at the airbase may be among those running? In any case, the ones who managed to escape death yesterday will be dead today or will die tomorrow running in the confusion of gunfire and the destruction preceded by the chants that welcomed the war. Zubaida now grieves over twin tragedies: the tragedies of her country and of her deferred dream. She has kept to herself the dream of returning one day to look for the copilots of his class, to ask them about him, to learn the details of his strange death, to find new photographs, and to reclaim the helmet that he wore flying the skies of Iraq.

She cannot remember the beginning of the letter. Did he write "darling" or "dear"? How did he address her in his letters? Although she used to swear that she knew his few letters by heart, she cannot now remember a single sentence. She closes her eyes to see the fine blue page filled with beautiful handwriting in green ink and to hear the beatings of her youthful heart, a sensation she will never feel again. In what dusty memory can she find his dear letters? On his return from India and after beginning his work at the airbase, he stealthily handed her a set of envelopes on which he had written his address. She can still see the Babylonian lion on the stamps he had affixed. He told her that all she had to do was to write a letter, place it inside the envelope, and post it in a letter box. But she had not written even a single letter. How he had implored! How he had longed to receive even one letter from her! She does not know where she left these envelopes after he had left the world, a lover dreaming of her braids and her eyes. She will live the rest of her life in the bitterness of his dream. She still keeps in her heart the address of his flight regiment. He was a young Iraqi, who had fallen in love with flying planes and who imagined that he had realized his great dream when he trained to fly the plane he loved. He told her it was a light English fighter plane and he talked profusely and with childish joy about the details of piloting that plane. She paid little attention to what he said and never took seriously the hints he offered about annoyances he was experiencing at work. In fact, she had understood nothing. Now, though, she would happily give the remaining years of her life for one hour of hearing him speak and for the opportunity to send him a single letter.

One afternoon, she sat at the front door of her house, a lock of her long hair tied with a thin turquoise satin ribbon, a shade of neither green nor blue. She wore a blouse of the same color. She busied herself talking to friends, in the hope that, on his return home that evening, he might see her. She had tried to run away from her passion by climbing to the roof where she could be all alone. She ran away from everything, taking refuge in making the numerous beds on the roof. She had volunteered for this job to escape the noise of the house, the chattering of children, the bright lights, and the doors permanently standing open. As she climbed the stairs, she could hear the sound of her heart beating hard against her chest, just at the thought of seeing his shadow on the roof opposite. She tried to follow the moving shadows reflected on the walls of the dim houses. After making the beds, she sat on hers, there where the moon had cast bluish silver rays. She raised her eyes to the sky in search of the bright polar star. Her friend Laila had advised her to talk to that star every night to express a wish. She still repeats the same words, imploring the star to make him think of her (Oh, evening star, as white as starch and as yellow as apricot). But he will never come back, and all her sighs of yearning are in vain. Only in dreams does he come, only in dreams. The dream slips from her eyelids at dawn, even though her lips may still be reiterating an impossible wish.

Her family sold the small house in which Zubaida had spent all her life. She felt then that her homeland, which consisted only of one floor, had completely vanished. When her family moved away from the alley, she began to invent excuses to return to the vicinity of his home. Once when she carried a piece of fabric to his house, so that his seamstress sister might make it into a summer dress, she learned that he had gone to India on an Air Force college scholarship. She trembled to think of him out of sight and so far away. She felt gripped by a pain so severe that she feared it might never leave her. The emptiness she experienced then soon engulfed her whole universe.

He came home parading in his military uniform, carrying in his eyes a dream that would never be realized. This was his last summer vacation before graduating. At its end, he was to finish the remaining part of his training. But it was during this period that the group that had killed General Abdel Karim Qassem came back to power. This time, they described their revolution as "bloodless" and named it the "White Revolution." She had not known then that his blood would make the revolution red. Only a few months later came the announcement that a group of young men were to be hanged on charges of collaborating with the enemy. The dead bodies were hoisted in Al-Tahrir Square, the Liberation Square, during a political celebration. The revolutionaries kept calling their coup d'état the "White Revolution," since hangings, after all, do not spill any blood. And so the men were hanged, and the revolution retained its pure white color. Zubaida had no wish to see the public spectacle in Al-Tahrir Square, but her secondary school took all the girls by bus to the square, to force them to rally in condemnation of the conspiracies wrought against the nation.

Zubaida stood among the crowd, looking at the scene, and not yet understanding the scale of the impending disaster. But she had a premonition that a catastrophe would inevitably follow and that the whole country would evaporate into thin air and turn into a bundle of light dissolving in space. She noticed that some of the people in the square were eating and laughing as they looked at the hanging bodies in the middle of the square. The speaker read out the death sentence using words that abused the idea of freedom. "Long live the nation!"

You speak out loud, sir, at the top of your voice and address the dead, forgetting that the microphone is sufficient to carry your voice far.

"Long live the nation! Down with the conspiracy!"

The crowds shouted, "Long live, long live," and "down, down, down."

All the hands went up at the same time on the orders of the leading party. Zubaida wished she could run away from this school gathering and from this frightful scene. She wanted to slip away without notice and without informing the school administration and the party establishment. A voice inside urged her to get out of the crowd, to move stealthily to a side street, and to go home. There, pack your bags and wait for the right chance to leave. The country had been tarnished and was in ruins.

Her friend said to her: "They're traitors." Although Zubaida did not feel like talking, she responded, "Yes." Now, as she recalls the events, she can see the whole picture more clearly: the crowds coming to witness the death scene without having had any evidence or proof; the flaunting of death in the square; the speaker who shook his hands in ecstasy and reveled on behalf of the nation, castigating the traitors and promising a similar fate to anyone tempted to betray the country. The amplifiers had been placed on electric poles, transmitting patriotic songs in celebration of the victory of the motherland, the failure of the conspiracy, and the inevitable death of the traitors. Zubaida's head ached as the crowds swayed like the lashing waves. The faces merged into a huge canvas of a mythical, colossal face, stretching and rippling across the length and width of the square. She felt exhaustion, nausea, and dizziness. She heard the speaker shouting and repeating phrases, the songs blaring out of amplifiers with jarring tunes, drums, and rhythms, the cheering crowds, the mouths eating and drinking. Suddenly the voices ceased, and the square fell as silent as a tomb. Zubaida had fainted. A schoolmate noticed her and dragged her away, telling the others that Zubaida was exhausted or perhaps terrified at the sight of the dead bodies, adding rather indifferently, "She has a weak heart."

One of the students sprayed some liquid from a bottle she had on Zubaida's face, stopped a cab on one of the side streets, and took her home. Zubaida gained partial consciousness while in the cab. Her face was pale. "Where am I? What happened?" she asked her companion.

"You must have been terrified at the sight of death," her companion said, "your heart is rather weak."

During that night, Zubaida fell ill with a severe attack of fever. Terror-stricken, she saw bodies swaying in the air, including the body of the husband of her geography teacher, who had been transformed through grief, anger, and oppression into a hard black mass. Her teacher was moving here and there, giving lessons to students who would never see her smile any more.

Before the hanging of her husband on charges of high treason, she had been a light-hearted woman who was very fond of wearing pink. The color added to the ruddiness of her cheeks. A happy person, she communicated a sense of relaxation and joy to her students. She never imagined that the day would come when her husband would be chosen as an example of treason, or that the authorities would use him to reaffirm their patriotism. The day after the death of her husband, the geography teacher looked dazed and lost among the maps of the oceans hanging on the wall and the thought of her husband dangling from a noose. Her smile had vanished, but she was too scared to change the pink clothes for the black, lest she get fired. As though to torment her still further, she was assigned to a class in political education. Although she was completely confident that her husband had never betrayed his country, she was forced to offer the lesson of death as a silent lesson in patriotism. Her smile disappeared, and her lessons became dull. The waters of all the rivers and oceans seemed to have dried up. Her body became emaciated, and she no longer cared for her hair. Then she stopped coming to school altogether, and nobody knew where she had been transferred, if indeed she had been transferred as the headmistress stated, or whether she had simply gone away.

The profound grief of the emaciated geography teacher and the sight of the young men dangling from the nooses in Al-Tahrir Square had left Zubaida in a state of shock. She felt a sense of bitter alienation, which she shared with her brother Ahmed. Thus began the first of Zubaida's impotent rebellions, this one against a reality she did not quite understand, apart from the image of nooses. Thus began also the dreams of freedom and departure, shared with her brother Ahmed. Together, they tore up the school textbooks and walked aimlessly along Sa'doun Street in Baghdad, looking for a Palestinian office, which was recruiting volunteers to the resistance that had become hugely popular after the Six-day War. It was a war that had left in its aftermath a defeat, shattering the first idols of generations who had grown up under the blazing sun of the Arabian deserts and had been filled with the illusion of triumph. People kept joining the ranks of the Palestinian resistance. They stood in long lines in order to travel and join the fighters whose posters appeared on street walls everywhere.

In the long lines, Zubaida and her brother stood and

waited. When their turn came, they stood in front of a young Palestinian woman sitting behind a desk. On the wall right behind her was the picture of a man whose head was covered with a Palestinian shawl. His face was concealed except for his eyes. He carried a rifle hoisted before his face. The radio amplifiers attached to the wall blared out a song, "This is my way, this is my way." The Palestinian woman told them that they had to attach two photographs to the recruitment form and that they would travel in a matter of days to Amman. Zubaida sensed that the woman had only pretended to be seriously dealing with them. She had not asked them a single question. In giving them the two forms and asking for the two photographs with such ease and indifference, had she wished to imply that they were unfit for the task? Zubaida and Ahmed left, dragging their disappointment with them. Had the Palestinian woman in fact accomplished her mission? She led them toward their first act of withdrawal. Joining the fight with the Palestinians was a very serious and dangerous matter, and perhaps they and she had behaved with inappropriate simplicity.

The atmosphere at home had changed. Even the nightingale, Sa'doun, did not sing any more but kept silent. It did not bathe in the water container inside the cage; neither did it spread its wings and toss the water up into the air so that it would fall once again on its head like rain drops. Father sipped bitter tea that evening instead of the arak. Ahmed went to bed early while Zubaida's little heart gave birth to an angry giant that she knew not how to deal with. From this great setback, a few small setbacks would be born that would become her intimate friends.

Who can write history? Who can write the stories of the little ones and the dreams of girls? Who can spread incense on the graves of loved ones?

Only the night comes to her in this friendless place, depositing bewilderment and expectation on her doorstep, then departs, leaving silence behind. The silence sings with a deafening noise; it smells of rain and tastes like bitter almonds. On summer evenings long ago, she was a little child with long braids and a bundle of dreams. She used to bend down to listen to her grandmother's heartbeat as she lay in bed on the roof. She used to check her breathing and count the stars.

Zubaida and Ahmed used to spend winter afternoons in their grandfather's room. At the farthest corner of the rectangular room, only slightly elevated above the courtyard of the house, stood a wide iron-black bed. Next to it, on a dark-colored wooden cupboard, a crystal-clear mirror reflected the light of the only lamp in the room. In the corner opposite the bed, a wooden cage held the nightingale, Sa'doun. Zubaida's grandmother chose the name herself.

Zubaida remembers clearly when Tahseen, who had left Ba'kouba to study at the Teacher's Institute in Baghdad, arrived carrying a small bag in one hand and a birdcage in the other. Tahseen was a slim and timid young man, coming from the orchards of Ba'kouba, carrying the scent of its orange groves. When he spoke with Zubaida, who was ten years his junior, his face turned the color of blood. On that day, she named Tahseen "The Warbling Nightingale."

In those days, Zubaida used to stand with her brother, Ahmed, waiting at the doorstep for the return of their grandfather in the evening. They used to run toward him so that they might carry his bag of apricots. One day Ahmed imagined that he saw him coming, though darkness had just fallen, and he could not properly see his grandfather's face. He ran and hugged the legs of a strange man. As he lifted his head to smile, he realized his mistake. The stranger understood the boy's dilemma and patted him on the head, smiling. Henceforth, Ahmed waited for his grandfather to come into the house so that he might see his face in the white light of the lamp above the house door. Over the years the bitterness of this first experience of disappointment diminished. Neither could remember many details of those days.

But one scene will always remain with Zubaida: grandfather's body lying on the carpet, covered with a cloth embroidered in gold threads, the women neighbors crying. In a dim corner of the room, her grandmother sat crying, her head uncovered. For the first time in her life, Zubaida was aware of the beauty of her grandmother's long, henna-dyed hair. The whole house was filled with grief. Only the nightingale, Sa'doun, was singing. Zubaida heard a neighbor say that the head of the corpse should not be lying on a pillow. A moment later, she heard the sound of her dead grandfather's head hitting the carpeted floor, the neighbor having dragged the pillow from beneath it. She could still hear the sound.

Suddenly, her mood shifts, and she spreads a large blanket over the debris of such early memories, covering them completely. Without any hesitation, she decides to postpone toying with their chaos, to forget about them for a while, recognizing that to defer action is the easiest and sweetest solution.

The planes unload their fiery cargo over the homes and alleys of Baghdad.

Residential neighborhoods are stricken with terror. The news reports that the dictator has appeared in the Adhamiya neighborhood. He appears on television greeting the people who gather around him. Although he tries to smile, the smile looks forced and artificial. His younger son stands by his side to protect him, accompanied by his private secretary who always appears with him. The scene lasts only a few minutes; then the dictator leaves the screen and the air raids continue to strike neighborhoods of Baghdad. Iraqi women, carrying their children, leave their homes and run.

The sight of grief-stricken women is not any different from the scene described by her grandmother, when Queen Alia, the mother of the young King Faisal, died. She was the wife of King Ghazi, who was rumored to have been assassinated because he allegedly sided with the Germans. The English killed him because they feared that they might lose Iraqi oil. On that day, a popular singer called Hudairi Abu Aziz sang a love song whose simple words asked: "This road, as you know, is slippery. How are you going to cross it?"

People understood the reference; they always do. It was a reference to the conspiracy that killed the popular king. The song was banned from the radio, but people kept singing it. Zubaida did not know the story of oil. She knew only that people used to buy kerosene from a cart pulled by a horse. Her mother used to fill a tin to feed the Aladdin kerosene heater, around which they gathered on cold winter days. When Queen Alia died, her weeping grandmother told her that she saw women go to the little streams branching off the Tigris, take pieces of clay from the river bank, and put them on their heads to show their grief. They tightened their *abayas* around their waists and walked, raving and weeping on the streets. According to her grandmother's description, it was almost like doomsday.

Will Zubaida tell others the stories her grandmother had told her? Will the homeland turn into nothing but memories? All that remains of Zubaida's father is a photograph she still keeps with her. He left the world as a sad stranger in the homeland that is now burning before her on the television screen. They are burning memories the way they set fire to a haystack. They are burning a land that stretches far and wide, a land full of trees and paradisal rivers. She goes out onto the balcony, wiping her tears away and seeking escape. Her neighbor is watering his potted plants.

"Look! Look!" he says to her. "This bee has found her friend in here, so she's staying with him. See for yourself that I'm telling the truth!"

The neighbor looks out of the balcony and starts to laugh. He continues his chatter, pointing to a woman walking on the pavement. "Do you know that this woman walks her dog every day at six o'clock sharp, not a minute earlier or later? Every day, she walks slowly with her dog, which looks a lot like her. Most people own dogs that look like them in some way. The varieties of dogs have increased a great deal because of crossbreeding, and there are now new and previously unknown pedigrees. Do you know why? There are farms for breeding dogs and experimenting with their pedigrees. These are huge farms run by the Russians in the area between Russia and Finland. Some of these dogs are extremely dangerous and aggressive by nature. You must have heard of the dog that ate the child in the city of Germersheim. In the past, the Russians exported their Communist ideas to us, created a Communist state in a large part of Germany, and turned this red zone into a prison for our people. And now after the fall of Communism, they are exporting those weird dogs to us. So beware of importing dogs from these Russian traders. The entry of such weird dogs into your country, Iran . . ."

"You mean Iraq, sir!"

"Did I say Iran this time also? I meant Iraq! You should beware of importing these dogs into Iraq."

As her neighbor speaks of people who choose dogs that look like them, she remembers her old neighbor Frau Schneider and her dog. Berlin was not the city that Zubaida had ever wished to live in, for she was first fated to live in the colorless, eastern part, ruled by prohibitions, fear, surveillance, coldness, and lethargy. People walked the streets like somnambulists, while she stayed wide awake even in her sleep. She received only a handful of letters every now and then, letters from her brother Ahmed in Tunisia. Letters to her family, however, were not possible, for she feared what the censors both here and there might do to them. A letter represented evidence of guilt for the family of a person who had chosen to live in exile. Like others in her situation, she heard of the chopping of palm trees and of the drying up of a land that had always had water.

When she lived among her Socialist women colleagues, she almost doubted the truth of the news about the war as relayed by Iraqi expatriates, who were lost in exile, believed by no one, and misunderstood and ignored by all. The international media's coverage of the war was short-lived. Mentioned recently, it was referred to as the "forgotten war." Zubaida no longer fears the apprehensions, or the ghosts that roam at night within the walls of her head, jump into her apartment, and keep turning around with her in the darkness of her room. She opens the window in their company to look out on the dark, dull street and watch people, deprived of their own will, wandering in the night in search of a breeze blowing from afar.

She used to be a little pleased that her brother in Tunisia was realizing part of his dream as a musician and teacher, although she in the Communist part of Berlin could not think of a dream. She was in a society that succeeded in guaranteeing bread to its citizens, but not the bread of freedom. As for Tahseen, The Warbling Nightingale, who had settled in Leipzig, the xenophobic Saxon city, she checked on him every now and then. He had never succeeded in establishing a relationship with a woman and remained locked up in his cage like a nightingale, singing sweetly whenever he felt imprisoned, bitter, or bored. He talked to her sometimes and visited her at other times when he felt like crying.

He talks to her on the phone, as she watches television and hears the news of the disappearance of the dictator and his entourage, and as the soldiers entering Baghdad look for them. Their photographs are printed on a deck of cards, a number assigned to each one of them, their names erased and replaced by fifty-four numbers. The telephone rings. The Warbling Nightingale, Tahseen, is at the other end of the line:

"What are you doing now? Any news?"

"Nothing, Warbling Nightingale!"

This was the way she had always addressed him, and he used to laugh. This time, he does not. Zubaida says to Tahseen, "It seems like you're crying, Tahseen!"

"Yes, but silently this time."

"I don't think there is any hope left! The dictator has been defeated as expected, but it seems to me that hope itself has also been defeated. We need to act wisely, Tahseen!"

"I'm going to commit suicide."

"You're kidding, aren't you?" She tries to moderate the significance of his words, adding, "Don't you forget to write me into your will! Especially for your fixed assets!"

"I'm not joking, believe me! How can a person live without a home country, especially when this country is impossible? That the home country should vanish into thin air is beyond endurance."

"Come to Berlin, Tahseen. This kind of talk needs a meeting."

Although she has tried not to take his words seriously, she feels very worried, all possibilities being open. She remembers that when the American army first entered Baghdad, an Iraqi engineer living in Damascus went up to the roof of an unfinished building and threw himself off.

Tahseen is no longer the same person she remembers, the one who came to Baghdad as a young man carrying a nightingale as a present for her grandmother. He has aged prematurely. Now with his stout build, his receding hair, and his rigid gait, he looks almost like a retired soldier. He has changed immensely. When he walks, he looks neither to the right nor left. Even when it is pouring, he does not carry an umbrella; he would rather die from the cold than wear a hat. He wears a coat that is big enough for two people. He does not know how to organize his residence documents, nor how to keep them in folders. His chaotic way with papers has created problems for him with the police. When he gets tired of all the official papers and letters, he puts them all into a bag, takes the train to Berlin, and throws them on Zubaida's table. She writes explanations on little pieces of paper that she attaches to each letter or bill. He neither smokes nor drinks alcohol. He fears going to the doctor in case he might hear that he has cancer. He'd rather death come unannounced. He dislikes watching football, likes following the news, and engages in very serious discussions. He is an only child, his mother having failed to provide him with a sibling. His father divorced her on this account and married once again, but having produced no other offspring, he died in a state of misery and disappointment.

Zubaida comes to, like a person coming out of a tired dream, but is overcome by a strange feeling. What if The Warbling Nightingale, Tahseen, were to commit suicide? What needless sorrow would overtake her? What would be her responsibilities in such a situation? She decides to travel to Leipzig and gets ready for the trip. She picks up the receiver and tells Tahseen, "I have business in your city, so I'll come today. Are you free to see me?"

"I'll wait for you at the train station."

Fires are filling the screen.

Zubaida stands in the train station. The trains disgorge departing people and devour others who gather around the train doors and enter. Doors close, and trains leave. The train departing for . . . the train arriving from. . . . Journey number . . . is two minutes late. . . . Zubaida does not know, nor is interested to know, from where they are arriving or to where they are departing. All she wants is for her train to come, so that she may disappear into it. Her loneliness adds to her self-consciousness, and it seems to her that all the arriving and departing travelers are staring only at her. She feels quite naked—exposed to everybody's gaze. It seems to her that all her failures and dreams are visible to other people, while only she respects the privacy of others' dreams and failures.

She gets on her train and chooses a window seat so that she can turn her face away from others. She hopes that nobody will occupy the seat next to her, since she wishes to talk to no one and for no one to talk to her. A tall fat man arrives, preceded by his paunch, and reeking of beer. He places his briefcase in the overhead compartment and prepares to sit next to her but changes his mind and takes the seat behind her. Before the train has moved, he is already snoring. An African mother carrying a child of almost two years takes the seat opposite. Zubaida feels uneasy because she does not wish to hear a crying child. But for some reason, the woman changes her mind and moves to the other side of the train. Now Zubaida feels comfortable. As the train closes its doors and begins to move, the seat next to her is still empty. For the first time today, she feels lucky, even if it is only for the space of two hours. She wants to look through the window at the horizon, but the window blinds are down.

She hoped that the train would be totally silent, that it would stop at no stations, moving on forever, an eternal train. She says to herself, "Take me to no-place, train of eternity." In a vision, her beloved pilot appears to her in his uniform, flying in the sky like a seagull, dreaming of her as she dreams of him. She awakens from this short reverie, not knowing that she has been asleep, the fat man behind still snoring.

At two minutes past seven, the train stops at Leipzig station, but The Warbling Nightingale, Tahseen, is not waiting for her. She thinks he may be a little late coming. She waits a little while, then calls him on her cell phone. The home phone rings without any answer. She expects that he must be on his way to her, or is standing somewhere in this huge station. This time she calls his mobile phone, but it is switched off. She waits for more than half an hour, but Tahseen does not appear. She sits at a nearby café, close to the train platform, so that she can spot him when he arrives. But he never does. She calls him for the third time at home, but there is no answer.

Zubaida anxiously reflects on Tahseen's personality and recalls once when he did not turn up for a wedding he had been invited to. He was at the time passionately in love with Zahra, who had married someone else, unaware of his passion for her. Tahseen had been living in the illusion that she loved him as well, and was shocked to hear that she and her family had accepted a young Afghan's proposal. Tahseen then fell into a severe depression and lived for a time in total isolation. He recovered after the wedding, which he had not attended, pleading illness. On the day following the wedding Zahra's father found him at home lying sick in bed. Tahseen apologized and pointed to the wedding gift lying at the corner of the room.

Zubaida imagines him tearful and silent at home, reconstructing an illusory love, which he had created by himself for himself, but which he could not turn into reality. This love, which he wished to keep as a fantasy, was the real source of his sadness.

Zubaida knows him well, for she was at Tahseen's house when Zahra's father arrived, and looked secretly at Tahseen when he was first introduced to Zahra's father. They embraced warmly, and it seemed to Zubaida that he laid his head on the old man's shoulder tenderly and for many seconds, as though revealing a love that he knew he was incapable of. He could not come to the wedding, for there he would have been unable to suppress his tears. Now he wishes only to keep walking straight from his house to work and back, looking neither left nor right, to work, without breaks, which might expose him, as Sundays and holidays now betray Zubaida. He will continue walking every day from his house to work and back, and every day one more hair will turn gray. He will grow older, but he will continue to walk in the cold city with the same upright bearing. The winds will blow away his illusions together with the falling autumn leaves on the streets of the cold city.

Sometimes the friend's sadness is too hard on the soul to bear, and Zubaida wishes she could interrupt his silence and cry with him. She would like to escape into other people's sorrows and, thus engrossed, run away from her own sadness. This is one way to play the game of hiding. She has spent years of her life running or keeping very still or skulking in the corners of life. From time to time, she imagines herself getting ready to return to reality, but mostly she stays suspended between heaven and earth, like Iraqi birds that fly away to escape the smoke and fire of the careless bombing and artillery shelling. She sees Tahseen clearly in her imagination living a passionate love story as though he were here in front of her. She looks for him among the travelers in the hope he will come to keep her mind occupied with the trivialities of life, while avoiding any mention of love, the fantasy of love, or the marriage of Zahra. He knows undoubtedly that Zahra's marriage has freed him from the problem of establishing connections with others, while keeping to himself the story of a love affair that will never become a reality.

Zubaida takes a cab to his address. She climbs the few stairs, stops in front of his apartment, rings the bell once, twice, three times, but nobody answers. She takes out a piece of paper and writes, "I waited for you a long time at the station, and had to come here myself. Where are you, Warbling Nightingale?" She fears he may have done something dramatic to end his problems. She goes back to the station and takes the first train to Berlin, enveloped in sorrow, and filled with disappointment and anxiety. A day, two days, weeks, and months pass. Tahseen never appears or calls her. Has he gone back to Iraq to burn with the country or has he left his home to live in a distant corner unknown to anybody?

In an insignificant section of a local newspaper from Leipzig, somebody reports that a man threw himself in front of a train and died. No identification was found on him to reveal his identity. It was reported that his looks suggested that he was foreign. She cannot know whether it was Tahseen, The Warbling Nightingale, or somebody else. She grieves even more on learning that the strange body had been cremated, the ashes placed in an urn and interred in one of the cemeteries without a tombstone.

She decides that she will also disappear now that The

Warbling Nightingale has escaped or vanished. She no longer has a friend to support her at a weary moment, or to discuss some decision. It is hard for any human being to exist completely alone. This is a living hell. She does not know why she has decided to travel to India, to the vast Indian subcontinent, to the warm rainy seasons that bring malaria. This is a daydream that dances with color. Two months are long enough for her to keep the new dream before she replaces it with another. How many times has she traveled in her mind! How many cities has she known inside out! Her head swarms with projects, like an archive or a cellar filled with old furniture and empty travel trunks. The owner of such junk cannot throw it away, discard some of its contents, or even dust its shelves, for fear that something valuable may be lost. Her head, like a deserted cellar whose contents are no longer usable, is infested with the green mold of decay. She is suddenly overwhelmed by thirst. The water here, however, does not quench her thirst, and the heavens show no tenderness. The stars do not shine, and nobody knocks at her door. No one at all.

At the end of every day, when Zubaida prepares herself for bed, her brain begins its daily journey. When her head falls on the soft pillow like a rock, the engine of her brain turns over and accelerates until total vertigo allows her to disappear from this world. Her night journey then begins, especially at the ends of days without daylight. For how many days pass when the darkness of day joins the darkness of night without interruption? Inside the head heavy on the pillow, the stars light up cliffs of distant cities, even when the moon begins to wane. Other cities stretch lazily in the spring sun along the banks of rivers whose waters are as red as clay. The rain falls on dry dust, while the scent of earth rises and drops of water dampen the pillow. Inside the head lying on the pillow, two rivers meet in a muddy flood coming out of her eyes. Inside the head lying on the pillow, soldiers march, hoisting severed heads on their spears. Inside the head, her city opens its gates to strangers. On the soft pillow, rain and grass and a head heavy with worries. Outside, a pigeon pecks on the window. The dream disappears, and the head sinks into the damp pillow. The morning has arrived.

She has entered her third decade in exile. The roots she carried in the only suitcase she took with her in the hope of planting them some place, any place, or taking them back to their original soil once she returned, no longer enjoy life in the dark soil. They have become creatures fascinated by the light. Open-eyed, they breathe the fresh air under the sun and drink the rainwater before it touches the earth.

CHAPTER
FIVE

Despair and walking will exhaust and drain her. She joins an angry, noisy demonstration, through the streets of Berlin, the city that experienced war, the blaze of fires, the destruction of history, the cruelty of the wall, and the bitterness of defeat. "Down with war." She knows that such protest is useless, for war will not be stopped by human protest against organized death. Thus, she finds herself protesting a war that she knows cannot be stopped, and, thus, her soul oscillates between despair and anger. Her throat becomes dry from repeating "down with war," and when she feels exhausted, she steals out of the ranks and descends stairs toward a small tunnel that connects two underground lines. How similar is this small tunnel to another in her soul. As she walks carefully through the tunnel, she spies a Russian violinist forced by need into this tunnel, where pedestrians throw coins into the hat he has left beside the small seat on which he sits when he gets tired of playing for those catching trains, not heeding Brahms's melodies or the Internationale. She remembers rushing, sometimes even leaping in elation some days as she crossed the tunnel, though on other days dragging her legs as though in iron shackles and tied to balls of solid steel.

She has become accustomed to watching the war on television without sound. She sees planes bombing houses and does not want to hear the sound, for sound scares her far more than the burning images. The telephone rings, and she picks up the receiver to greet an artist who expresses his alienation and madness in unique paintings.

"I have painted a picture inspired by my burning country. I want only one spectator for this painting. Could you be that spectator? Creativity needs an artist, the look of art, and an audience. I have the first two and need the third component."

He begins to laugh, and then she hears him weep. She says: "I'm coming over now."

When she enters the studio, she sees several huge paintings all inspired by one idea: intertwined shades of red paint, shapeless in form. In the center of the studio, on a wooden stand, he has fixed an exceptionally long, rectangular painting, also in red and its derivatives. On its right side, in a triangle he has painted a white horse, without a rider. The painter, seated on the floor for there is only one chair in the studio, asks her to sit opposite the painting so that she may view it thoughtfully. He is quiet as she looks at the painting.

She says, "Is this a horse that has returned after losing its rider?"

He nods in agreement and says, "The horse returns alone, sad, to his family."

The artist is quiet, and silence reigns in the studio. Zubaida moves among paintings, all of them very similar. She sees Baghdad in them, recognizes details easily even without clear features of the city. In one painting splashes of paint intermingle violently. The painter says it was inspired by an explosion that occurred the day before near Al-Nasr movie theater in Baghdad.

Yesterday on television, Zubaida had seen some Iraqi soldiers hiding behind sandbags near this movie theater when the explosion took place right next to them: They did not leave their position, save for one, who left his to check for casualties, then returned to his colleagues. Not one of the soldiers had budged from his position; in fact, the screen had shaken from the magnitude of the explosion. She remembers Al-Nasr movie theater but she never really liked it as she had the one at Adhamiya. There is no place in Baghdad like Adhamiya. Al-Nasr movie theater is now closed because of the explosion, and beside the theater a barricade of sandbags shield young men carrying weapons, who don't even have time to wash their faces. Where could they wash up? When a soldier emerged to announce that there were no casualties, the camera recorded his face, and she read in his eyes the absurdity of the death awaiting him.

"Yes, sir, everything is ready for combat," the same phrase repeated by the commanding officers of the platoons and regiments when television broadcasts the farcical meetings of the dictator with army commanders on the eve of the war. A commander could not even tell his leader, "We are short of equipment, gear, and ammunition, sir. We are lacking clarity, sir." Everyone had to say to the glorious, soon-to-be-victorious leader, that everyone is prepared for this battle. And the leader would, in turn, praise them, saying, "Well done, God bless you." They would stand one after the other, announce their names, the names of their platoons, saluting smartly.

They would then stand behind the microphone and speak, the dictator asking them all the same question: "Are you fully prepared?" And the officer would answer: "Yes, sir, we are ready for battle, prepared to sacrifice for leader and homeland."

"Do you require anything for the upcoming battle?"

"No, sir, we are fully prepared."

As she watched this scene of army officers meeting with the dictator, Zubaida saw them headed toward inevitable death. She believes that a great loss is about to befall her homeland, and she reads this in the features of all soldiers. She knows they are lying, and that none of them is fully prepared, and that, as they salute the dictator, they are taking leave of him, without any regrets. They know he has humiliated them, but how is a soldier to balance between his duty to defend his homeland and his desire to reject the dictator?

When Zubaida turns around to look at paintings on the opposite wall, she can no longer see the painter, and the door of the studio is ajar. She feels slightly frightened, thinking of the artist's anxious, edgy character. He is a man who pours all his energy onto the canvas; who runs in the streets at dawn; who usually avoids other Iraqis; and who phones every once in a while for months, and then not for a year.

She decides to leave the abandoned studio. As she walks through the studio she hears her footsteps echo. She leaves the door open. On her way back to her apartment, she continues to ponder: "Why would the painter leave his studio and leave me alone with his paintings when he had invited me to visit him?" Zubaida assumes that his behavior reflects his anxiety. She then wonders whether he will ever return. Would he throw himself under an approaching train? Would he jump off the high-rise? Would he make himself food for the whales? She lifts the receiver and tries to call him at home. The telephone rings, but there is no answer. She waits an hour then calls again, and again the telephone rings, but there is no answer. At midnight she hesitates to call but decides that the case justifies her calling at this hour. Still there is no answer. She knows that he often refuses to answer phone calls, but this time seems different.

The next morning she leaves her home early and takes the tram line to the artist's apartment, on the ninth floor of a pale-colored building. Because of her claustrophobia, she often avoids using elevators for fear that they might break down with her confined inside. She climbs the stairs, resting a little on every landing. During her climb to the ninth floor, she meets some of the tenants leaving their apartments who ask whether the elevator is out of order. On the ninth floor, she stands in front of the artist's apartment door, left open exactly like that of the studio. She rings the bell, but he doesn't appear, although the doorbell can be heard clearly. She tries a second and a third time, but he doesn't appear. A woman across the hall opens her door and tells Zubaida that when she returned late last night, she had found the artist's door open. As Zubaida begins to descend the stairs, the woman tells her that the elevator is working, and she answers: "I know that." She feels certain that something has happened to the artist, that his extreme, almost irrational sensibility must have led him to a destiny he had designated for himself in one of his paintings.

The war will end one way or another; in one death or the other. She feels a profound fear as she looks into the faces of people who talk to correspondents of news agencies and satellite stations: They speak real words about worrying expectations. They are simple folk talking about the closing of horizons and the ambiguity of what is to come. They use simple and clear and more articulate words, distinct from the phony, selfish, and misleading language of politicians and intellectuals. Only ordinary people recognize the truth; only they stand at the doors of their ruined houses and speak honestly. In the corners of their houses one can see pots, baskets, and the remnants of clothes on a wooden or iron bed in a courtyard near a palm or orange tree. One can see also a grandmother asleep on a bed just like one on which Zubaida's grandmother used to sleep, when little Zubaida looked up at the sky and counted the stars one by one. Is it possible to count the stars, or even watch them, amid the smoke of fires and bombshells? Everyone speaks of an imminent disaster, and the politicians alone speak from within elegant rooms with the Iraqi flag mounted behind them, declaring that a beautiful tomorrow will bring happiness to people. They speak and their minds have different projects and deferred departure plans.

Zubaida sees two tanks on Al-Wathba Bridge that connects the two banks of the Tigris. She sees planes bombing in the direction of Karkh, where there are government headquarters, but the two tanks on the bridge remain silent, produce no artillery fire. Perhaps the commanders have escaped to a place far outside the capital, and perhaps the capital of Al-Rashid, Baghdad, has been left without guards, soldiers, or police. She wonders, "Where are the enormous numbers of security men who used to drag the innocent to ghost houses?" Prisoners, no doubt, remain trapped inside the strong vaults, locked in by prison wardens who took with them the maps of the underground and the keys to cells. People say they hear wailing, but cannot find the entrances to these legendary vaults.

Zubaida remains bewildered, fixed in her place, wanting to escape and not knowing where to go. No, she knows no one. She recognizes people but doesn't know them. They may know her and not know her. Flames devour the houses of Baghdad; its streets are deserted, and the two tanks on the bridge remain silent. A capital city has never before been conquered by two tanks on a bridge; bridges are usually demolished to prevent an enemy from advancing.

Suddenly, without thinking, she rushes to the bathroom and washes her hair as if she were cleaning away the ashes of fires. She puts on her black coat and leaves her apartment, walks to a flower vendor, buys a bouquet, and gets on the tram. She descends and walks alongside a long fence, then pushes open a huge, old, rusty iron door and enters a cemetery. She heads toward a grave in a corner near a tall tree, the grave of the German writer Rolf Richter with whom she had a close friendship. She puts the small bouquet on his grave and sits on the ground. At once she feels serene, her soul soothed. She has fled from images of death and destruction, with all their fearfulness, to find solace in a death that had tasted of freedom.

Richter was a German writer, painter, and cinematographer who lived in East Berlin. Because he was considered faithful to East Berlin, he was permitted to travel. It was not easy to travel in Richter's world. The state viewed him as a faithful Socialist, whereas in reality he suffered from the absence of real freedom, which for him meant the freedom of others. Despite the fact that the government had provided him with all the necessities of a decent life in East Berlin, he used to long, extraordinarily, for the Middle East. He would always express joy whenever he could travel to Baghdad, for him a very special place. Baghdad, from which Zubaida has escaped, and continues to long for and escape from again, the city she loves and fears is Richter's city of magic and beauty. He would feel depressed the day he returned to East Berlin and saw the snow accumulating on top of houses. He had not finished his novel, which had become a pile of papers that needed someone to go through, to read his reflections and his search for freedom and for another place. It was, perhaps, Richter's obsession with that other place that had shaped a special, beautiful, and strong bond between them—in a place in which they both felt strange. Richter departed quietly, without preliminaries; he died in the first months when Berlin was quietly cutting and discarding its iron shackles. Richter did not die in war, but because of it; not in socialism, but because of it; not at the wall, but because of it; not in the snow, but because of it; not in death, but because of it.

She moves her head closer to the grave and sets about talking to him calmly: "My dear friend Rolf, I am sitting close to you now, a little higher on the ground, equal to you in exile, wiping freezing tears from your cheeks, sharing with you a warm smile, and weeping for you and for myself. I tell you they are burning the city you loved, they are burning your Baghdad and you don't know it. This city that I promised you I would return to, that I would never forget. Whenever we met, you used to repeat, 'Don't ever forget that you will be going back. Hold on to your dreams and never abandon them.' Baghdad is burning,

my friend. Forgive me, I had to tell you that. I am being faithful, for how was I to hide such a secret from you and leave you
in the dark? You may blame me later on."

As she speaks, Zubaida feels small drops of rain, and her
mood saddens. How could rain falling from a sky that was not
her own ease her state? Once, she had been close to a person
who loved the Middle East and especially Baghdad, the Baghdad she left burning on the television screen in her apartment.
In a few minutes, she departs, thinking, "Farewell, dear friend."

Zubaida enters her apartment, opens a drawer, and takes
out her passport. She studies it carefully and flips through its
empty pages. It holds no statements, no stamps, for she has
never used it. Once she wished for a passport like this one; to
open doors to the world she had dreamed of, but this passport
has never opened even one door. It was merely a number of
empty pages in the shape of a small notebook with a red cover,
incapable of opening the door of a single city outside her world,
a world shaped like a closed circle. She sets the passport on the
table and turns to look at the suitcase that has long stood on top
of the cupboard. She pulls the suitcase down and, with a wet
cloth, wipes the dust, then washes her hands. She sets the suitcase on the bed and opens it, looking intently into a black space
glittering inside, vast and deep. The two belts that could hold
clothes firmly inside seem to be holding back her freedom. She
stares at the suitcase for several minutes, but doesn't put a piece
of clothing inside it. She sits beside it silently as if she were vis-
iting a dear patient in a coma from which there is no hope of
recovery.

Zubaida lies down on her bed in a small hotel in Amman, listening keenly to a distant call for prayers that cuts through the
silence of the universe in beautiful piety. Her eyes look toward
the window, waiting for sunrise, waiting for the birth of a Middle East morning that she misses and fears. Then she walks in

the blazing sun, enjoys listening to ancient songs and the news in Arabic coming from an old wooden radio. She grows accustomed, once again, to the week that ends on Friday; her soul delights in the celebration of the Prophet's birthday; and she relishes the taste of the extra sweet afternoon tea. Hundreds of small, familiar things come back laden with the smell of perfumed dust. Evenings have a different color, and the Arab moon is as sad as she knew it the day she had to leave. In the beginning, she had given in to bewilderment and nostalgia, and in the weeks that followed these days, the questions became magnified and the contradictions of her life increased inside her as she realized that she no longer knew which city she longed for, which city she really belonged to. Although she knew that torn roots can neither be fixed in an alien earth nor even replanted in the land they were uprooted from, she still carries them around in her purse wherever she travels. Still, she continues to hope that she may return to her homeland—there—to feel whole again.

In Jordan, Zubaida sits on a bench in a public garden and buys tea in a plastic cup from a young Arab who has a master's degree. Like her, he is a stranger in the huge, Arab world. He wants to add a mint leaf, which he pulls from a nylon bag in his pocket, but she requests that the tea remain black and clear, unscented.

The young man asks her:

"Have you come from Iraq or are you going there?"

"Neither."

"Please allow me to ask a question. Why are you here? I like Iraqis—that is why I ask questions of them."

"I came here because I long for the Middle East. I live in a cold city. I came to see the sun, hear my language, drink tea, and watch the moon, the sky, and the stars. For here the moon, the stars, and sky have a different color."

"Gracious God, madam. Here the prophets were born, but, please excuse me, here, too, murderers were born. I think the murderers were born even before the prophets, and that is why the prophets came to counsel them and to spread love. Allow me to introduce myself. I am Egyptian. I have a master's degree in history, but because I found no job opportunities in Egypt, I came here and ended up selling tea. I honestly wanted to change things; it was not only the need for work that prompted me to come to Amman. I wanted to change my life, to go from one place to another. Man is prone to boredom, madam, and thus must diversify life so as to avoid falling into the trap of a tedious existence."

The Egyptian at first refuses to take money from her, but finally accepts when she insists. She walks crooked streets on several hills surrounding the city whose lights seem familiar and make her yearn for paths she has abandoned. For a second, she thinks that the evening would be beautiful were it not for the silent sorrow that dwells in her eyes. As the old color comes back to the evening, certain words, as if scolding her, resound in her ears: "Man is prone to boredom, madam, and thus must diversify life so as to avoid falling into the trap of a tedious existence." Why had she fallen into such a trap? Here is the Middle East, Zubaida, roam around in it, take your fill of its air, quench your thirst with its water, and enjoy all its inherent contradictions: the sun, the shade, the light, the shadows. In the city of snow, you know no contradictions, for the shade has no sun opposing it and even the shadow has no existence. How can shadow exist without light? She has escaped from the darkness and has come in search of the warm sun. Here, she sees things in their real colors, smells the aroma of oranges, and sits under trees that spread their shade over the walls of houses located at the edge of mountains. In her illusion, her feet lead her to paths and streets she does not know, to secret borders where her childhood and adolescent years once emerged from the caves of the Middle East under the scorching sun, but she does not recognize them now.

The following day, she goes to the bus station from which

buses travel to Baghdad. At that moment she decides to go to Baghdad. She stands watching the platform crowded with passengers and with people seeing others off. In the midst of noise and dust, as if she were pulling herself together and getting ready to leave, she stands there. She has no suitcases, no one to see her off, and no one to whom to say good-bye. She feels touched by the curiosity of the Middle East, a curiosity immersed in a dream and mixed with the dust of roads. She feels dizzy. One of the buses fills up with passengers, and only a small barrier separates her from it. Next to the other bus, a man collects passengers' passports and glances at her occasionally. She doesn't look as if she is going to join the travelers. A black headdress slides off the head of a woman in black—the black that frightens her. Nevertheless, Zubaida rushes to help her, lifts the abaya, and smells in it the scent of the shrines of imams and holy men lying in memory, and sees in it ancient, forgotten vows. The Iraqi woman says, "Thank you, my daughter."

"Have you been here in Amman for long?"

"No, not really. I came with my daughter; she is here to continue her education. The truth is, my dear, I was worried about her, what with the increasing number of hooligans in our country, I tell you and I trust you. Which city are you from?"

"Dear aunt, I came from Berlin. I left Iraq a long time ago, but I am bored with the cold and snow there, and so I came to smell the scent of the Middle East. I get so tired of the cold and the fog."

"The cold and the fog are much better, dear girl, than privation, which leads man, God forbid, to disbelieve in God." The Iraqi woman's tears pour down. She dries them with the side of her gown, wipes her nose, and continues: "They took my husband from home and led him to a place we do not know. Nobody can know where they take people whom they decide they don't like. He has not returned since, and I do not think he ever will. We have only this one daughter. My brother-in-law works in Dubai, and he is sponsoring her here until better times come.

Stay where you are, dear girl, don't return to Baghdad. I saw you looking at the bus and something inside told me I must advise you against going back. Go somewhere else if you don't like the place you are living in now. Young men have been taken to wars, and they have brought other Arab citizens to work in their stead, and women are left without men. Young women have no suitors, for young men are driven into war, then come home in coffins. And those who escape are executed. I swear to you in the name of Allah, they executed our neighbors' boy and brought him home in a sack; they knocked at their door, gave them the sack, and asked them to pay the price of the bullets they shot him with! People are terrified, my dear girl. Do you have family in Iraq?"

"I, too, have a brother on the front, dear aunt."

The woman opened a paper bag and took out a kaleeja, a pastry filled with dates, and offered it to her, begging her to eat it. Zubaida hesitated, but the woman insisted upon sharing it with her, and so Zubaida ate a piece. The woman said, "If you have a letter for, or a request of your family, I am ready to go to the address and deliver the message. Don't worry; I swear I will go to your family wherever they are, even if they are outside Baghdad."

"Thank you, dear aunt, I have already sent them a letter with a friend who left a few days ago."

"I saw you watching the buses as if you were looking for someone, or wanting to travel."

"No, dear aunt, I only wanted to see you all."

As the bus driver approaches and returns the old woman's passport, she rises from the stone bench. Zubaida stands also and extends a hand to the woman, but the woman kisses her enthusiastically.

For an instant Zubaida forgets the years of exile, the long estrangement, the strange, cold cities, the other languages, the pale complexions, the summer rains, and the foreign passport, and stands watching the bus leaving for Baghdad, traveling with it in her mind. Her soul travels, and her body remains fixed on the pavement as the bus departs, then disappears. When the pavement gradually clears, the man standing at the barrier, worn out by curiosity, asks her without preliminaries: "To Baghdad? There is another bus in a few hours."

She awakens from her reverie, and without thinking she says, "No, not yet, I just left it yesterday."

The Middle East at night is a completely different world, one almost kind to strangers. Millions of stars glow in the sky of this city, and the lights of the small, white stone houses glimmer from a distance. Streets in Amman rise and slope like sea waves under the tires of the fast, yellow cabs. At ten o'clock on a warm night Middle Eastern in temper and geography, Zubaida stands on the side of an asphalt road, waiting for a taxi. A cab stops right in front of her; she opens the door, gets into the back seat, indifferent to the driver's glances, which take her back to times she loathed and forgot. She tells him: "To the Luweibda Mountain, please."

Through the mirror, she observes the driver's eyes and sees the curiosity trying his patience. She laughs secretly, and ignores his unspoken desire to talk. The driver wants to convince her to move to the front seat because he is not used to a woman riding in a cab alone at so late an hour. Neither this, nor his questions concern her: "Are you Iraqi?"

She doesn't reply.

"Are you a Muslim?"

She doesn't respond.

"Muslim?"

"Why do you want to know? If you are hinting at the issue of the veil—*al hijab*—yes, I am a Muslim. I got into the car to enjoy the view of Amman at night, please."

"Excuse me, but I'd guess you are living in a European country. Many come here after they get bored. European countries only offer depression. It is true that we live here with great difficulty, but life goes on, thank God. Ultimately, man doesn't die of hunger, but could certainly die of cold and loneliness. Death in exile is very difficult. Even the rich, when they get older and feel that they are nearing death, come back to their homeland. How will one be buried in exile? Living in exile is possible, but dying in exile is unthinkable. It is heartbreaking."

"I don't disagree with you."

The driver stops talking when he recognizes that she does not want to continue the conversation. She is enchanted by the glittering city, by the stars and the lights. She has never imagined that Amman was so close to Baghdad; distances seem vast when the soul is still young.

She wakes up at dawn in her room in a small hotel in Amman to the sound of the morning call for prayer. She wants to walk the streets of Amman as the sun begins to rise, but before she gets out of bed she closes the suitcase, and the city disappears inside its black, empty cavity: The stone houses, trees, people, taxis, and buses going to Baghdad all dissolve; the pavements, pedestrians, and cafés evaporate; and the streets remain trapped within the shiny belts of the hollow suitcase. She wakes from her dream. She removes the dream and hangs it on a hook beside her coat as she usually does whenever she returns from distant cities, islands, and ports. She returns to her thoughts and illusions. She feels satisfied by the silent, still dream, and convinces herself that patience is sweet and that waiting for more beautiful adventures, more distant travel, more dazzling cities, and an impossible greater love, is sweeter still. She forgets Time, trapped in her suitcase and mocking her.

She has heard travelers tell many stories of Amman, that beloved, spacious gate to the now sad Baghdad, the gate that, for a long while, has been the only station and meeting point for the banished, lost, and fugitive Iraqis and their families. From the stories of such travelers, Zubaida knows the routes, the places for drinking tea with them in the squares and gardens. She has traveled there from her balcony, and she has loved the journey. She weaves a lovely, golden shawl from these stories and wears it over her black coat. She wraps herself in the shawl, creating a refuge from cold and estranged, long nights.

The suitcase is empty, and Zubaida is paralyzed. She has traveled without the suitcase, as travelers do, when they use only their imagination. She realizes, at this moment, that she has been asleep inside this suitcase for a long time. She feels overwhelmed by fear and thus locks the suitcase and returns it to its place on top of the cupboard. She fears looking at it, fears her other—her imprisoned, defiant self—and its potential rebellion.

CHAPTER
SIX

She draws the sun's rays from withered, wet chestnut leaves and braids them as she once braided her youthful hair, hid it in her old pillow, and then left it on the bed under the sky in that first house. She had come to live at this center of the city after the collapse of the wall that had divided it for decades. Alone, she had celebrated the end of a smaller exile within the larger one, once she could move freely from one residence to the other. As she moved into the heart of Berlin once again, Zubaida realized that this area looked very much like Adhamiya. Having lived against her will in another apartment for more than two long decades, she now believes that returning to this particular place was motivated by an old yearning.

Here, on her balcony, the snow falls in July. She collects it in her hands and makes a snow-white palm tree that does not thaw. She hangs all her old wishes on its palms. Today she cannot understand her denial of self through those long years and her acceptance of things as if they were indisputable facts, for she knows she is a rebel by nature. Here her imagination blossoms again to create fresh fantasies adorned with timid threads of hope. Time moves slowly, feeding her doses of patience which she gulps down in order to endure its slow passage and brighten her spirit. She removes the stifling shroud so that she may breathe again, sends a kiss across the air, and leaves the apartment.

For a moment, nothing here seems to remind her of the place over there. She does not know which button in her thoughts will open up large gates into the past, releasing the specters of people she knew long ago. In fact, she cannot remember many of their names. Zubaida travels on modern trams, sits in their seats, and looks through glass windows to the streets. She busies herself trying to learn their names. When the tram carriage happens to be almost empty, she opens her handbag and transparent specters of people stream out and sit silently around her, occupying the empty tram seats and traveling along with her. When she gets off the tram, they do not go with her but remain in their places. A voice whispers in her ear, "Don't worry! You'll find us when you get home." This experience recurs, and although she tries to discover its meaning, she cannot. Instead, she loses herself in all its various meanings. After years, here she is still searching for beginnings. She is conscious of these last years. She feels particularly resentful that a hair dye will no longer cover her gray hair. She resents the hairdresser who tells her in confidence that the nature of one's hair changes over the years and that she will need a stronger dye to change the color adequately.

Then, one day from the balcony adjacent to hers on the eighth floor, a man fell and was killed instantly. She cannot truly remember him, for she had met him only a couple of times on the elevator. He used to greet her courteously and avoid talking with any of the neighbors. She wept long when the woman living on the ninth floor told her that her neighbor had committed suicide because he was lonely. She does not know why old absences and losses surface in her memory at this moment of a stranger's death. Also, she thinks, tomorrow is detestable Sunday when my e-mail inbox will be empty. Zubaida tries to comfort herself—she invites comfort, and so it comes creeping into her heart. Her sorrow diminishes, and her pains become bearable. She slumps on the old sofa, and immerses herself in elegiac music. During the long autumn nights, when the rain falls heavily, she unplugs the phone, switches off the light, and listens attentively to the music merging with the heavy rain lashing against her window, until she falls asleep. When feelings of loneliness and separateness from the universe overwhelm her, she wakes at sunrise and does not budge from the sofa. There she waits for the universe to play its symphony for her alone.

She knows that Sundays expose her shame and betray her sorrow and loneliness to strangers. In the stillness of Sundays, she pretends to be working and active, and tries to turn this activity into a source of hope. Or she sits over a cup of coffee in some imagined break, trying to revive some old thoughts of joy. She begins by preparing her suitcase for a journey of the mind. She has rejected all the familiar forms of travel because she hopes to travel to especially lovely locations. She trains herself to keep her memory intact. She recalls for no apparent reason some boring, even worthless, details that are too useless to store. She does things perhaps out of the fear of oblivion, the archenemy of memory, or out of the fright that sometimes comes over her as she tries to retrieve the names of familiar faces coming out of her head, from her huge store of memories, or from the heavy load that she drags behind her.

Often she sighs in relief. After the towering thick wall had collapsed, she had filled her lungs with a fresh breeze without even realizing the enormity of relief that would follow the collapse of this wall as though it had been made of cardboard without any foundation. Nobody witnessing this event would be able to forget the ease with which the nightmare had disappeared, or the simplicity with which the ugly gray fence had come down. Although the wall had not represented an obstacle to her own movement, its existence had allowed her to judge harshly those defending it, who were also strangers to the city and its history. They had defended the barbed wire and slept undisturbed by the sounds of automatic weapons. They felt no shame for the shackles curbing the freedom of others, even though they were running away from injustice and aspiring to freedom. In fact, they found in this division and in these chains a victory for their own ideology, which they carried with them like a charm and before which they bowed down as though it were an idol.

The First War, the one with Iran, seems remote, forgotten, absurd, and long gone. The only evidence proving its existence personally and specifically is a letter she received a few years too late. It told of a little boy she knew who looked like her. She had said good-bye to him in silence the day she left in a hurry. On that warm afternoon, she had left him playing football barefoot on the muddy street and had waved good-bye to him from a distance. The boy, who became a soldier, was taken by the war and forgotten in a pit. The letter said he had been in Al-Faw and that he had forgotten to get up and go home. She cannot find the courage to utter his name, because she feels that a hand will reach out to wrench her heart, and she knows that she cannot endure that pain. She cannot imagine him a grown man. Her memory refuses to change the last image of him in her head. She even imagines that, if she went back to that muddy street, she would find him there as he was then, a small boy playing happily and waving to her, this time welcoming her return.

Belated sorrows have their own special flavor, unlike new, hot sorrows that come all of a sudden, brandishing their sharp swords, cutting off a piece of the soul, and leaving the fresh wound to settle down until the body gets used to the pain and accepts it. Belated sorrows are like an ancient, dark-colored creature with a pungent smell like the vinegar her grandmother made from ripe dates and left stored to distill slowly in huge bottles in the dark cellars. A small quantity was enough to push the spirit to the edge of hallucination and nausea. Nobody knows exactly what happened. The soldier went and never came back. Soldiers go and never come back. An old story. Zubaida braids the old stories and places them in her cupboard, hiding them among her clothes, forgetting them there. On desolate nights, one story comes out of the wooden drawers of the cupboard followed by others. The characters in each tale dress up before they knock on the door of the cupboard to ask permission to enter her room, one after the other. She sits transfixed on the leather sofa, as a spectator might sit alone in a dark auditorium, gazing intently at the lit stage and following the same theatrical presentation again and again, despite the loss of all sense of awe. Nothing is left except the emptiness and the repeated questions that remain unanswered. Adventures may bring some relief, but she never dares to venture. She sits and watches and observes and waits.

Zubaida stretches out on the heavy leather sofa in the drawing room, unable and unwilling to move toward her bedroom to sleep. It is two o'clock in the morning. The television is off. Before her are the reflections of distant buildings. Another light on the window comes and goes like the pendulum of an old wooden clock standing in the courtyard of the first house at Adhamiya. Her blind grandmother used to count the strikes to know the time herself without having to ask. She was a proud soul. Zubaida does not know the source of the movement, for something might be moving on her neighbor's balcony: a plant or a little tree moved by the wind with a source of light or lamp concealed by the twigs and leaves behind. When the wind blows, the light returns dancing and sparkling on her window. She watches the monotonous, alternating movements of light and shade, which keep her awake. She covers her face and remembers the coffee-colored blankets of her childhood and early youth. The blankets conjure up memories, and, one specter invites another: her father's picture, her mother's picture, the workers in the large blanket factory, the streets of the Adhamiya neighborhood where she once lived, her first school, the royal cemetery, the cold water tap, free for passersby and fixed in an opening in the wall of the cemetery garden. She drank from that tap every time she walked by. The pictures in her head crowd and intertwine themselves without any logic. Enveloped in darkness, she stares so hard at the dimness that the holes in the texture of the woolen blanket turn into passages full of little moving masses the size of pinheads. People and dolls and trees and pictures of actors. All the past with its jarring, contradictory, and harmonious images overlap before her without chronological or logical order.

She thrusts the covers away from her face and feels overwhelmed by the repeated shadows and lights reflected on the window. She wants to draw the curtain in order to rid herself of the reflections, but she feels too heavy and too bored to get up to draw the curtain, and too paralyzed to fulfill her dormant wish to leave the living room and go to bed in the small room. Her body refuses to obey, so she stays in her place. She turns around and pushes her head into the pillow so that she might not look through the holes of the woolen texture of the blanket, whose passages are growing larger and turning into endless alleys. She cannot sleep. When she stops herself from staring at the window to avoid the tedious repetition of the scene and looks instead at the tiny holes of the blanket, she is assailed by the sounds and rhythms of the repeated war song on television, saying, "Let the men take charge." The song and the rhythms of drums echo in her ears. The voices of the choir singers resonate as they chant monotonously and without any enthusiasm; dressed in military uniforms, their heads draped in head covers, they carry guns. The drumbeats pound so hard that her head turns almost numb.

The war has moved into the radio and television studios. At the same time that Iraqi military personnel are leaving their camps and abandoning their locations and barracks, the singers, the chorus, the chanters, and the actors are singing in military uniform. She feels that the battle has turned into a battle of songs. But she knows that the whizzing sounds of the Apaches will drown the voices of all the singers in the world. Is there a betrayal in the country? Is it treason against the dictator or treason against the country? A perplexing question.

A few days earlier, she had joined tens of thousands of people marching against the war. But these remain only voices that exert no power over the military decision made by the powers that control the world, whose arsenal of continent-crossing missiles and planes sail through skies and cross oceans. What is her voice in the midst of the roaring demonstration? The demonstration over, everyone went home. The Germans went to the pubs to have a beer, and some of them bought wine and went home. They would meet with neighbors or lovers and talk briefly about the war. The policemen who guarded the demonstration, lest rioting should break out, took off their iron helmets and went home to play with their children.

What about Baghdad at this moment? What piece of news will it wake up to hear? When will the dictator be ousted? When will the game end? They had warned him last year that he would not celebrate his next birthday. In twenty days, his birthday will have passed. Was the timing all that accurate? The fires raged through the whole of yesterday as the forces accelerated their march toward the Iraqi capital. Do they wish to put an end to the dictator's power and regime on his birthday? At night, she watches demonstrations on the screen. Zubaida knows that demonstrations will become only a passing item on the news, for the war continues and Iraqis' deaths are a fact repeated daily.

Footage of another demonstration in the British capital appears on the screen, headed by an old Iraqi woman. For a moment, she imagines that she recognizes the face, and tries to retrieve the name from the archive of memory. Suddenly, the geography teacher springs before her, the woman whose husband had been hanged during the early days of the return to power of the dictator's party. Is she the same stricken woman who opposes the war because she knows the difference between the fall of a nation and that of a dictator?

Zubaida falls into a short slumber, awakened by her worries and the insistent pounding of the repeated war song that echoes in her ears between wakefulness and sleep. She wakes early in the morning and lifts the blanket. The lights of buildings and streets are gone, and the movements of shadows and light have disappeared from the window. She wants a cup of coffee to change the taste in her mouth. She has a strong urge to smell the coffee, her strongest motive to get up. She hastens to the kitchen, takes out a packet of Arabic coffee, fills the coffeepot with water, and adds three seeds of cardamom to the boiling water in addition to two spoonfuls of coffee whose strong smell refreshes her. She leaves the dregs to settle, then pours the coffee into a cup decorated with Eastern designs. She takes it to the living room and lies on the sofa, half covering herself with the blanket when she feels the cold air. She feels warmed up and takes a sip, enjoying the coffee, which she likes without any sugar, preferring and loving the taste of its bitterness—the bitterness almost of first love.

After she takes her third bitter sip, she glances at the black television screen and reads the blackness as Baghdad, a city shut off, its image gone. She feels suddenly terrified. The coffee cup trembles, spilling a few drops onto the blanket. She gets up and cleans the blanket with warm water. Seated again, she wraps her trembling body with the blanket once more. She is no longer able to drink the rest of the coffee, feeling sickened by the empty television screen, which, she is convinced, is her only window to Iraq. For almost a year now, it has transmitted nothing but images of Iraq and especially Baghdad, drowning in a sea of expectations and possibilities: death, annihilation, destruction, burning oil, the smell of gunpowder, the remains of dead bodies, and the wolves coming from the border deserts to devour the corpses of soldiers and non-soldiers alike. She cannot bear to look at the pictures of Baghdad burning, and is equally terrified by the image of Baghdad dead and still. She presses the "on" button on the remote control, which lights the screen, showing an area of debris and a man wearing a gray dishdasha saying, "They bombed our homes and our neighbor here is dead, his kids injured. This side of my house has collapsed. No government officials were here."

A subsequent briefing reports that the dictator, accompanied by his private secretary and one of his sons, was actually in the house next door, but nobody knew it. He had moved to that house at night to meet with some of his advisers, but the Director of Intelligence had not turned up for that important meeting. The dictator had the feeling that his head of intelligence had betrayed him by informing the American forces of the whereabouts of the meeting. So he had left the house with his companions and disappeared unnoticed.

The Minister of Defense sits in the basement of the Ministry of Defense. In front of him is a primitive, tattered map, which looks as though it dates back to the preprinting era. He explains the military situation to some of those present. His face does not communicate conviction that his forces are in fact capable of stopping the invading armies. He knows his words will convince no one, for he himself does not believe them. He moves his hand and points with a stick to the locations of enemy movements, and the locations of Iraqi forces moving to attack the enemy from several points. But the movement of the stick over the map does not impart any conviction, and neither does it prove the presence of Iraqi forces. The minister does not mention the name of the dictator, the customary way of paying homage to him. Is this conscious or unconscious? Has he forgotten or has he tried to forget that omitting the name of the dictator as the architect of the imaginary victory can lead to his death? Perhaps he knows that the dictator could get into his car at any moment and head toward the desert to vanish. He could walk with the caravans and Bedouin nomads in search of food and water.

At that moment, a bomb hits the building of the Ministry of Defense. Debris falls into the cellar, and the map moves from its place. The minister remains calm, as required by the military code of conduct, and continues talking as though nothing has happened. His stick points to the battle between his army and the invaders. While the stick points to these events on a tattered map, on the actual ground, there are no soldiers, officers, or military ranks.

Zubaida follows the events from the distant place in which she has been seeking her own peace. On the screen she sees seven military personnel running away, even as they remove their military uniforms. Three black bulletproof cars pass in a hurry, while the Minister of Information waits for the dictator at the entrance of the television studio to record a talk in which he will call upon citizens to resist. But the cars do not stop to let the dictator out. The minister feels that the country has fallen into the hands of the invaders, and that the dictator must flee in one of those cars. The minister of Information replaces his green uniform with a suit, says good-bye to his guard, and leaves for an unspecified location. The newscaster stands alone in front of the camera and improvises, since he has not received material from the minister, who has just run off. The director repeats the same song, transmitted endlessly during the war, "Let the men take charge." Nobody stays in the studio except the director, the cameramen, and the newscaster, since they are all unaware that the officials and the guards have fled after seeing the minister enter dressed in military uniform and emerge wearing civilian clothing.

The bombing intensifies, and the bombs fall near the television building. The bombs avoid the building itself in an attempt to keep the transmission going until such a time when it will be needed to relay messages to the people after the invaders assume control. The song is repeated again and again, arousing the patriotic feelings of soldiers who know nothing of the escape of the dictator and his entourage in three armored cars to the out-skirts of a distant city. Eventually, the continued desperate resis-tance pushes the invading forces to bomb the television building in a bid to stop the transmission. Thus the newscaster, the direc-tor, and the cameramen do not merely leave the studio but the whole noisy world as well.

The dictator's words are hollow and meaningless as he speaks to the leaders about the war, the enemy, and his military plans, he whose knowledge of military stratagems and tech-niques has never exceeded the green uniform he wears and the decorations recording imaginary victories. But his status forced army commanders to salute him as supreme head of the army. For this reason the Minister of Defense, who had been explain-ing with his stick the movements of the invaders, now sits alone in his room, locking his door, and refusing to see anyone for half an hour. During this interval, he sits on the sofa in a corner of the room, with the Iraqi flag folded beside him. The wind coming through his window, which ruffles the flag a bit, also carries the smell of gunpowder. He looks at Baghdad burning, and starts to cry. When he feels a bit more calm, he asks his guard for a cup of tea, then sits down and writes a letter to the dictator, imploring him to arrange a meeting quickly about the military situation. He gives the letter to the guard and asks that a special messenger be allowed to meet the dictator's guard to deliver the message. The special messenger leaves in haste, but asks the guard not to stay in that room but to head for a secret location, for fear that this site might become known. He had heard rumors about the betrayal of some regiment commanders and of their cooperation with the invading forces. The Minister of Defense gives his flag to the guard to carry with him to the other secret site.

But the guard says, "Do you think it's necessary that we carry this flag with us wherever we go? After all, we will be moving a lot these coming days! And then, there is a small flag on the table in your new room. It's just a symbol, be it small or big."

The Minister of Defense kisses the Iraqi flag and puts it back on the chair, but he cannot stop a tear from falling.

The guard notices and says, "Are you crying, sir?" The commander says, "When men cry, it means that the disaster is unspeakably serious."

Barely has one hour passed before the messenger returns. He is silent for a moment, salutes, and the minister realizes that he has had no access to the dictator.

In dismay and frustration, the messenger says to the minister, "I couldn't find the president at the arranged place. I've tried in vain to find out where he is, but they left absolutely no hint as to where they have gone. I think he left for somewhere unknown."

The minister signals to the messenger that he wishes to be left alone with his guard. He gets up, and walks back and forth in the room.

The guard asks him. "What do you think, sir? Do you believe that our president has fled somewhere?"

"I think so! Get me a car that has no military signs and let's inspect the sites."

The minister drives the car himself, with his guard at his side. He tries to reach the area close to some military sites protecting the capital. But he hears the sounds of bombings. When the guard turns on BBC radio, he hears the newscaster say that

Baghdad International Airport has fallen into the hands of the coalition forces after bloody battles that have left a large number of Iraqi soldiers dead. This was a ferocious battle for the occupation of the most important strategic location controlling the Iraqi capital.

The minister turns back and heads for the road leading to Al-Kut, the location of the largest Iraqi army camp. On the way, he sees scores of American tanks heading toward Baghdad, which could only mean that the camp has also fallen, and so the communication line with the president has been cut off. It is not clear whether he has fled or whether he is dead. It is not wise for him as a minister to appear in his military uniform, his very appearance having become dangerous. It is also difficult for him to appear in civilian clothes when meeting with fighters. He doesn't know that there are no soldiers left in these sites. The minister is about to head home when his guard suggests that they go to a private home on the farm, a reserve used for security reasons only when necessary.

The three cars accelerate through the main roads leading to the city of Al-Ramadi. There the president and his entourage exchange their cars for a pickup truck loaded with cargo as camouflage. They are followed by cabs, which had been loaded earlier with boxes full of dollars, and the convoy sent to an unspecified location. The president's women, daughters, and children are sent to different locations. The soldiers have no idea that their leaders have deserted them, and continue to believe that they have to obey orders to stand firm or face the penalty of execution. The president sits next to the driver in the pickup truck, wearing a Bedouin *abaya* and dark glasses. The decorations have left his shoulders, and he is celebrating his birthday on the twenty-eighth of April. This was the American president's promise to his people: that the Iraqi dictator would not celebrate his next birthday.

The dictator president has fled to an unknown location, so the news broadcaster says, although only some believe the news while others remain skeptical. All the power that has kept the country and its people in manacles, flaunting its authority to prevent people from breathing the fresh air of their own country, dissolves like salt in water, as do all the figures of the regime who had struck terror in the hearts of the people and induced nightmares at night when their names were mentioned or their pictures seen.

Some soldiers fire at a convoy of tanks but are immediately shot at and killed by tank fire. Fighter planes bomb camps, and the sounds of huge ammunition explosions bury terror-stricken people. The bombing extends to other large cities beyond Baghdad to prevent the army from moving toward the capital. Television cameras show young soldiers marching out of the big camp in the city of Mosul, even after its commanders have run away and left them without support or sustenance. Their military boots are tattered, and some of them are barefoot. They are walking along asphalt roads in the middle of valleys and plains, hoping to cover the distance of hundreds of kilometers to reach their towns in the south, crossing the whole country from north to south on foot. These are the forgotten soldiers. They ask the cameramen for some bread and water, and call out to cars to stop and take them home. But nobody listens to the defeated soldiers, for the defeated are voiceless.

The Minister of Defense looks at his soldiers walking barefoot, hungry, and humiliated. In his secret refuge on the outskirts of the Iraqi capital, he watches them on a small screen, but he does not speak. His guard looks only at him. The minister no longer has his military rank since he is no longer a leader. The guard is no longer a guard. The minister and his guard have become two defeated individuals.

"The president is stupid, and a coward, too!" For the first time, the Minister of Defense says out loud these words that have haunted him each time he has been alone.

Suddenly the American CNN shows people removing chairs, vases, and small oil heaters from ministerial buildings. An elderly man appears on the screen holding the dictator's picture and banging at it with his shoe, screaming at the top of his voice, "This is the man who destroyed Iraq! O people! O world! Here is the man who destroyed us, destroyed the country!"

The minister repeats his statement to his guard as though talking aloud to himself, "The president was stupid, and a coward too! I've known that all along! You may go home now! Baghdad has fallen, the country has fallen, and its fences and protection are down. The army has fallen, and so have I!"

"I will stay by your side, sir!" the guard says.

"I'm no longer the commander here, for we both have the same rank! Two soldiers united in defeat."

A citizen climbs the base of the dictator's statue in Al-Firdaws Square in Baghdad. He tries to smash the statue, but his axe is too weak to destroy the steel-hard statue built on a sturdy base. Soldiers in an American tank standing on the side watch the crowds waiting for the toppling of the statue. But the citizen's axe cannot smash it, and his efforts produce nothing more than scattered splinters. An American soldier who has been standing on top of the tank climbs the statue. He wraps the American flag around the face of the dictator, ties a rope around his neck, and fastens the rope to the back of the tank. When the tank moves a bit, the dictator's statue falls down. A small crowd gathers, hitting the statue with their shoes and dragging it through the streets of the city.

Has the road back to childhood and youth become strewn with flowers after the disappearance of the dictator? She knows quite well that the dictator will not shoot himself in the head, since he has never known shame, nor ever will, as evidenced by his own history. The minister who felt depressed at the sight of his starving, barefoot soldiers does not have the courage to shoot himself in the head either. Zubaida herself does not possess the courage to admit that her view of her country has now become much more painful. In the past, possibilities existed for her return, even though they depended on various decisions and resolutions, but all such possibilities now seem remote. The fall of Baghdad has closed the gates on her rebellious soul. She once wished she could surrender to the spirit of the place, barren or fertile, intact or broken, large or small. But now she stands in alien territory. All she possesses is a booklet called passport that carries her photograph, the date and place of her birth. It allows her to move to other places, even though she is now incapable of any such movement.

The huge bronze statue fell, preceded by others. It will be followed by countless others in the same way that Berlin's wall had fallen while the city survived. Berlin, the city she both loves and hates, has survived. Ambiguous feelings bind her to this strange city, which is changing, growing healthier, and regaining its splendor. It is a city always on the go, never stopping. It is a young woman who washes her face every morning in its icy river, which flows at the foot of the building in which Zubaida lives. Berlin will remove the remaining barbed wires from its streets. Zubaida thinks of Baghdad and wishes she could learn from Berlin how to love life.

The residues of hope have faded from Zubaida's spirit, having dimmed a bit when she left home as the dictator turned the country into his own home. She knew that the dictator was no more than a single person and that dictatorship has always needed only some watering to bloom and appear clearly on the streets, and in schools, institutions, and homes. The collapsed statue, dragged down with the help of an American tank, had made the crowds happy once again. This always happens whenever an idol falls, signaling the beginning of anarchy on the streets and fueling a desire for revenge. Many questions begin to worry her, more vexing now because of her state of sharpened consciousness. All her doubts have disappeared and all the ambiguities as well, since the long years of experience and disappointments could not allow further doubts or possibilities. When hope fades away, energy dies, and the spirit feels weak and exhausted.

Sitting alone in the living room of her apartment, she keeps fiddling with the satellite channels. But no songs can inspire her soul, nor can the old cherished movies make sense to her now. She doesn't like watching the news any more, since the images of death are always the same. The images of fires seem like replicas of earlier fires, all the tanks look the same and spew the same fire, and the soldiers' green helmets and clothes are all exactly the same. Only the familiar streets have changed, for they are now filled with military fences, barbed wires, and barricades. Movie theaters have switched off their lights, leaving nothing but the unlit signals. Theater curtains have come down, leaving only a bare stage.

As though talking to herself, Zubaida says, "I've chosen stillness and given up movement. Would it be possible for me today to start afresh? Could I throw away everything around me: the fridge standing at the corner of the kitchen like a policeman preventing my leaving prison, the washing machine, and the old furniture? Could I prepare myself for walking the streets of a new town? Would it be possible for me to throw away the closet? It has not been left to me for safekeeping. No woman entrusted it to me like the woman who had left her cupboard with my grandmother."

The papers on which she has recorded her fears and her

longings for freedom suddenly emerge out of her computer, rolling into the room, she feels, out of a distant past, settling in front her, and bearing all the details of her life. She has written these down for her own benefit, hoping that they might leap back into life once recorded on paper. She needs to become reacquainted with her story and to read what she has written. She wants to conjure the past, to feel the present state, and to record the impossible dreams she has been longing for, in a manner similar to a confession before a priest, hoping it brings her some relief. But it proves useless.

For days on end, she continues to write. She produces neither tears nor emotions. Throughout, she feels rather as though she were recording someone else's confession. Still, she continues to shed her own skin and stand facing herself, debating and recording the minutest details. This becomes her daily routine until in the end she feels she is facing a flawed history, though she may not want to blame herself for all of its errors. She tries finding a balance between patience and inaction, luck and possibility, between forgetfulness and awareness, between desire and impossibility, between attentiveness and lethargy, and between understanding the facts and justifying them, but she reaches no conclusion. She looks at the manuscript she is producing, and feels that she is playing with her history once again. Still, looking at some of the facts terrifies her, and she fears that she may have been cheating the priest or the judge inside her. As the rain falls heavily on the glass door of the balcony, she scatters her pages on the balcony floor, so that the rain may wash out their flaws, the anarchy, and the remorse. As soon as she feels that she has wiped the past clean, she gathers the papers again and throws them into the dustbin, realizing that history cannot be revised once it has occurred.

Zubaida sits and sips her tea, then sips it again, and for the fifth or tenth time finds it tasteless in her mouth. A photograph of her father, wearing a cap like King Faisal used to wear, sits on one of the shelves of the bookcase. She had taken it out of the photo album, intending to give it to a photographer to enlarge and frame so that she could hang it on the wall before her as a symbol of integrity. But events have grown larger than the photograph and the frame, for they have covered a whole nation. If Zubaida were to go back to Baghdad, she would not know her way to Adhamiya. She remembers the day she saw crowds of people running and lynching a human corpse that looked blue and seemed a strange amorphous mass. She remembers how the man who carried a knife in his hand had dug with his teeth into his dishdasha.

It is eleven o'clock in the morning when she hears an ambulance stop near her building. In answer to the intercom, she presses the handset button connecting her to the front gate. A voice tells her that an elderly woman had called them on the phone, but when they rang her bell, she did not answer. They are worried she might be in danger or she might have died. Zubaida presses the button to unlock the front door and let the man in. Afterward, she hears the doorbells of the adjacent apartments, followed by a ring at her own doorbell. When she opens it, the ambulance driver greets her, saying apologetically, "An old woman called us, saying that she was in danger, and gave us this address. But when we rang her apartment bell at the front gate, she did not answer. That's why we had to ring the bells of all apartments, but it seems nobody is in the building except you."

Zubaida is aware that nobody is in the building except for her and the old woman. Everybody else goes to work, but she is unemployed. She says to the ambulance driver, "I think the woman who called lives on the seventh floor, Apartment 3, but she is hard of hearing and may not have heard your ring."

The ambulance driver thanks her and goes down the stairs. She closes her door. A little while later, she hears the ambulance leaving. She does not know whether the woman opened the door for them, or whether, in despair, they decided to leave. At that very moment, she feels deeply lonely in this tall building.

She is the only foreigner, the only unemployed foreigner in this tall building. No friends visit her, and she has lost the skill of welcoming guests. Few are the people who are like her, and few are those in whose company she feels at home and to whom she can talk freely.

She does not want to watch more images on television. Instead, she reaches out to the bookshelf, takes her father's small photograph and looks at him in his vest. She talks to him, saying, "Stand by me, dear father, even in your grave. Give me a little strength and a lot of patience to face life. I can't bear talking and I can't bear other people and I can't even bear myself. I have grown old, father, and age has its limitations, because when one grows old, one sees the world differently, sees with painful clarity all the details, the flaws, and the shades that used to seem rather hazy in younger years. You gave me bitterness, so give me strength as well, father."

She repeats these words in a trembling voice, kisses the photograph, and returns it to the bookshelf. She starts to cry silently. She now wants to lie down a little to rest. She places her head on a pillow, but does not close her eyes. Instead, she stares at the ceiling of the room, and at the three lamps attached to the aluminum column. Still lying on the bed, she reaches out with her hand to switch on the light and then to switch it off again for no obvious reason. She looks around the place, getting lost awhile in the black shelves in her room laden with files recording a part of her history, papers and letters from German authorities, and bank statements always arriving loaded with debt. She feels hungry, so she decides to indulge her stomach. She gets up and goes to the kitchen, but she finds nothing appetizing there. She opens the lower part of the refrigerator and sees some frozen meat. She takes out a piece, looks at it, then returns it to its place, feeling quite sickened by everything. She finds a red radish, which she takes and begins to eat to fill her empty stomach. She leaves the kitchen and goes back to the living room. Feeling in need of some cool air, she opens the window and takes a deep breath. But when she feels the cold stealing into her body, she closes the window and sits on the sofa.

This is not the first time that her heartbeats have felt irregular. A month before, while on the metro train heading home, her heartbeats accelerated and she felt cold sweat pouring down her forehead. She cannot remember what happened to her afterward. She found herself in some hospital's intensive care unit. After doctors had tested her heart, she learned that she had fainted on the train and was rescued by passengers, who had called an ambulance. She was given the address of the person who helped her so that she might thank him if she so wished. When the tests had been completed, they gave her some advice and asked whether she wished them to contact her family. She told them that her family was in Iraq. When they asked whether she had any relatives or friends in the city, she said, "Nobody."

She left the hospital.

Her tired heart urges her to think hard about her condition, but only the image of Beirut leaps into her sight. This was the city she has always dreamed of, even during the civil war. But she could not make up her mind even then to attempt an adventure as others did. She knew that either they came to regret it or had the satisfaction of having at least tried. A vague decision begins to shape itself in her mind, even though fear remains uppermost. The objects around her grow in size and hamper her from thinking through her decision. The cupboard and the washing machine grow larger, while the fridge lengthens. The books bulge, and the television turns into a wide cinema screen. On the screen is a southern woman, calling for her daughter who lives in exile in some remote country, saying to her, "Enough of exile! Come back. Living in exile will kill you."

Zubaida has the feeling that the call is meant for her. The building seems to her to shake as though hit by an earthquake.

She realizes that the tremors are inside her head and that she has to sit down, relax, and think about her decision. But her heart beats irregularly once again, and she is overcome with fear, now that she knows she is alone in the apartment and in the building too. She writes down the number of the ambulance on a piece of paper, and she lies down on the living room sofa, covering herself.

Every night when she covers herself in bed, she remembers the woolen blankets produced by the factory where her father used to work. Every night she has a vision of her father coming through a long corridor, and the pores of the blanket turning into long corridors and passages peopled by friends, her pilot lover, her mother, her grandmother, her geography teacher, and the old neighbors. She used to turn right and left in bed, feeling sleepless, and becoming drowsy only at dawn.

She would wake up to the noises of buses on the streets of the city, and would say to herself, "I've knocked on all the doors of the world, but the world has never knocked on my door, not even once. The days here are drawing closer to the sun, but I cannot find my shadow here on earth or on the walls or the balcony. I have left no shadows on this foreign land. I have almost shed my skin and I feel cold as though the sun's rays give out no warmth, as though the laws of physics have no power over my tired body or over my heart, whose accelerating heartbeats wake me up suddenly in the middle of the night. I don't know, but something inside me seems to grow gradually, something that the rules of oblivion or physical decline do not apply to, something that defies death and disintegration. A fire settles in my soul and in every particle of my being, and in every part of my body. I stand up and throw the window wide open. Scattered sprinkles of rain enter, blending with an eternal and voiceless moaning. An angry giant emerging from memory walks before me, raising his finger like a Greek god, and reiterating his threats of everlasting torment. This is the evening curse, the juncture toward which I have been pushed by the hand of fate. This is the fever that will never subside; this is the state of hallucination. I feel that an impending danger is knocking at my door, and peering stealthily at me through the window when I sleep."

Her heart beats irregularly, and she grows rather scared. She has always yearned for salvation, but whenever salvation seemed to come, fear moved ahead, and whenever fear receded, salvation through death approached. She hesitates to call the ambulance. Some resistance still remains as well as a sense of strength and a belief that she may just be suffering from temporary boredom and depression. Or it may be a feeling of oneness with the world, a state where the private and the public unite. In the past, whenever she had felt particularly sad or afraid, she would call the mad painter, The Warbling Nightingale, or the sad German writer. But they are all gone now. She asks herself whether she still has the courage that has helped her to last this long or whether her loneliness signals her refusal to change.

Her heartbeats become even more irregular. She feels alternately cold and hot. She wipes the sweat pouring from her forehead, suspecting that this condition is similar to her experience on the train more than a month ago. She takes up the receiver, calls the ambulance, gives them her address, and hangs up. Wavering between wakefulness and sleep, she feels almost drugged, and many images pass in front of her eyes. She dozes off a little, then wakes up a little. Time passes, and her heart swings between calmness and tension. Fear suddenly vanishes; she feels a new serenity. She no longer cares that the building is empty. What does it matter if the old woman on the seventh floor may have been picked up by the ambulance a few hours ago? Who cares?

The doorbell rings. Someone is ringing from downstairs wanting to enter. She has neither the strength nor the desire to get up. The bell rings again, and again she does not get up. She hears the bell ringing in the adjacent apartment on the eighth floor. It keeps ringing in several apartments on other floors. It keeps ringing here and there in the hope that somebody may open the building door for a person to enter. But all the apartments are empty. She gets up, goes to the window, and opens it. She leaves it open to let in the air wet with rain, and goes back to lie down. She dozes off and falls asleep.

AFTERWORD:
THE STATE OF EXILE

Zubaida's Window is a novel of Iraqi exile. It is also a novel about painful history and contemporary tragedies in Iraq. The pain and angst of the female protagonist Zubaida seeps through and outside the pages, leaving readers at times mystified and bewildered; at other moments empathetic and in despair. This is not an easy novel to read either in style or content. But Iqbal Al-Qazwini manages to capture the sense of alienation and paralysis experienced by millions of Iraqis throughout the world who have not only found themselves forced to flee their homes, but have been watching the destruction of their country from afar and in great despair.

Through the fragmented and partly repressed memories of her main character Zubaida, Al-Qazwini gives us a taste of historical events in Iraq leading up to the most recent invasion in 2003 and the ongoing occupation. Her description of Berlin, Zubaida's place of exile, provides an interesting and very specific background to the experience of forced migration and exile. Zubaida's emotional journey contains a damning critique of a socialist system—in this case the former German Democratic Republic—a system the protagonist experiences as gray, cold, hypocritical, and soulless. At first residing in East Berlin, Zubaida lives through the German transition to a unified city and country, although she fails to achieve for herself a sense of belonging in Germany.

Zubaida's Window is not simply about the physical and material realities and hardships related to living in a strange place away from home. Exile here also refers to a state of mind and being. Received notions and ideas as well as set practices and traditions are unsettled when people are forced to leave the known and the familiar behind. While many of those exiled face a "crisis of meaning" (Al-Rasheed 1994, 91), others fervently and desperately hold on to the past and everything they knew. Zubaida experiences both: a "crisis of meaning," sometimes bordering on the surreal or even madness; at the same time, she fervently holds on to her memories. She tries to control them, to nourish them, at times to block them out.

Zubaida is not only a passive victim of circumstances; she is also a self-imposed exile, built around her mind and body. The ritual of making and drinking tea or coffee, as she used to back home, might seem a banal everyday activity. Yet in the context of Zubaida's detachment from her current physical surroundings and within her inner life of memories, the physical acts of making and drinking tea represent not only continuities with the past but also possibly life-saving acts. And despite her great sense of alienation and despair, Zubaida's resilience allows her to outlive many of those she cares about who give in to hopelessness.

Not surprisingly, the author, Iqbal Al-Qazwini, is an Iraqi exile herself who has lived in Berlin since 1978, following her departure from Iraq. She was born "by coincidence"[1] in the ancient city of Babylon—one of the historical centers of human civilization—when her family was on a three-day visit. The family returned to Baghdad shortly after her birth, and according to Al-Qazwini, her sense of "inner diaspora" started from there. She studied English literature at the University of Baghdad from which she graduated in 1976. Like many educated and politically active urban women of her generation, Al-Qazwini became involved in the Iraqi Women's League, one of the largest Arab women's rights organizations of the day. The League, which had close connections to the Iraqi Communist party, sent her as a delegate to the Women's International Democratic Federation (WIDF) in East Berlin in 1978.

Soon after her arrival, Saddam Hussein became President of Iraq early in 1979 and the crackdown on the political opposition, including members of the Iraqi Women's League, worsened. Al-Qazwini was unable to return home and has lived in Berlin ever since, and was there when the city and country unified in 1990. From 1978–1990, Al-Qazwini worked as the editor responsible for the Arabic edition of the quarterly journal *Women of the Whole World*, published by the WIDF. During this period, she also became a noted freelance journalist for various Arab and German media: Her articles have appeared in *Asharq Al-Awsat*, the most widely circulated Arabic daily; *Al-Rhyad*, another newspaper; and *Transnational Broadcasting Studies*. Most of her writings address women and gender issues, human rights, child labor, and intercultural exchanges. She has also worked as the editor of the quarterly journal of the German organization for Human Rights in Berlin and has been involved in supporting and campaigning for asylum seekers in Germany. In 1993, Al-Qazwini was elected to the International PEN World Association of Writers. *Zubaida's Window: A Novel of Iraqi Exile* is her first novel.

The contemporary context of the novel is the U.S.-led invasion of Iraq, beginning on March 18, 2003. It took three weeks for the Iraq government to collapse, which is fictionalized toward the end of the novel. While the main character, Zubaida, is trying to come to terms with the current context of war, violence, and devastation, she makes it clear that in her view the destruction of Iraq started decades ago. Through Zubaida's imaginary travels in time, Al-Qazwini propels the reader into Iraqi history, starting with the revolution in 1958, which turned Iraq from a monarchy into a republic. Then there are references to the first Ba'thi coup in 1963, which deposed the republican President Abdel Karim Qassem, followed by a second Ba'thi coup in 1968 referred to in the novel as the "White Revolution," which started 35 years of oppressive Ba'thi rule. The eight-year-long war with Iran—from 1980 to 1988—during which thousands of Iraqi and Iranian men and women died, constitutes another historical segment in Zubaida's memory of the past.

Before explaining some of these historical references, a note about memories and the construction of Iraqi history may be useful. Memories, whether individual or collective, are not static and frozen in time, but live, rooted in the present as much as in the past, linked to aspirations as much as to actual experience. Different accounts and interpretations of events may usually be inspired by particular world views and frames of mind. My own research into the modern history of Iraqi women recognizes that experience, memory, and truth do not necessarily overlap, that multiple truths may surround an event without diminishing either the significance of memory or the importance of finding out what "really" happened in terms of political developments, repression, wars, and social changes (Al-Ali 2007).

In the aftermath of the invasion in 2003 and the escalating violence and sectarian tensions, as well as the contest for power and to create a national identity, history becomes a powerful tool. Narratives about the past control different attitudes toward the present and about the future of a new Iraq. Such narratives will relate to claims about rights, about resources, and about power. More crucially, different accounts of the past may lay down the parameters of what it means to be Iraqi, who is to be included or excluded. History may justify and contain narratives of unity and narratives of divisions and sectarianism. History may justify an invasion and ongoing war as well as condemn it (Al-Ali 2007, 3-4).

While the fictional character Zubaida and her family

perceive the end of the monarchy and the revolution in 1958 as the beginning of the end of Iraq, memories and perceptions about the 1958 event differed greatly among the Iraqi women I interviewed for my book *Iraqi Women: Untold Stories from 1948 to the Present* (2007). Although many women I spoke to pointed to the political repression, social injustice, and the gap between rich and poor as characteristic of the monarchy prior to 1958, many women (and indeed many men of that generation), like Zubaida, remembered the King and that time with great nostalgia. I expected women from the former political elites and upper-class backgrounds to reminisce with sadness about the "good old days" of the monarchy. But perhaps it was not surprising, considering what followed, that many women of modest social backgrounds remembered the relative social and political freedoms people enjoyed under the monarchy. Some women I talked with acknowledged that they have revised their views and attitudes toward the monarchy in light of the severe political repression and suffering experienced over the succeeding decades.

But many Iraqi women I interviewed think of the 1958 Revolution as a positive liberating event. What started out as a military coup d'état by a small group of officers in the early morning hours of July 14, 1958, soon turned into a full-fledged revolution. Masses of people crowded the streets, celebrating and expressing their support after hearing one of the leading Free Officers, 'Abd Al-Salam 'Arif, declare the existence of the Republic of Iraq on radio. Members of or sympathizers with the Iraqi Communist Party, one of the largest political parties at the time, generally describe the Revolution with great enthusiasm. Those women described the day as "the happiest of their life" (2007).

Memories about the shooting of members of the royal family, the hanging of political leaders and the display of executed members of the ancien regime, which Zubaida remembers, evoke contrasting feelings among ordinary Iraqis and scholars of the modern history of Iraq. Some have argued that, given the strong anti-British sentiments of the day, the violence associated with the 1958 Revolution was relatively contained, certainly in comparison with what was to come (Farouk-Sluglett and Sluglett 2003, 49). Yet women across the political spectrum mentioned the violence that took place in the first days of the Revolution.

It is important to point out that prior to the revolution most Iraqis, especially girls and women, did not have access to education and struggled to survive under harsh economic conditions. While social injustice and exploitation led to social unrest and later on to the revolution, an increasingly politicized class of educated young people also wanted total independence from Britain, as well as a more just social system (Al-Ali 2007, 66).

Despite occasional incidents of prejudice and sectarianism, Iraq in the 1950s and 1960s was for the educated middle class a multicultural and to some extent cosmopolitan nation, which encouraged education, travel abroad, and cultural appreciation. References to multicultural and multiethnic Iraqis run through the novel as Zubaida describes her childhood fascination with the wedding rituals of the Mandaeans, for example, a religious minority in Iraq (also referred to as Sabaeans).[2] Her best friend at school was Leila, part of a Kurdish family from the north of Iraq. Cross-ethnic and cross-religious friendships, relationships, and even marriages were very common among Iraqis, obviously contradicting some of today's reports of sectarianism as an inherent element of Iraqi culture. Al-Adhamiya, the area of Baghdad Zubaida grew up in, is the center of her memories of a diverse, multiethnic, and multireligious society. Although predominantly Sunni, Al-Adhamiya was a mixed and tolerant environment in which Zubaida felt at home. It is in Al-Adhamiya that she falls in love with the young man who became a pilot.

Although relatively popular among the general population, Abdel Karim Qassem ruled only for five years before he was deposed during the first Ba'thi coup in 1963. The coup was staged by Ba'thist and Arab nationalist officers, like 'Abd Al-Salam 'Arif, who had been one of the Free Officers with Qassem in 1958. Unlike 1958 though, the coup did not trigger support from significant numbers of the population. On the contrary, masses of people poured out onto the streets, expressing their support for Qassem and fiercely resisting the coup, especially in the poorest neighborhoods. The level of violence in the immediate aftermath of the coup in 1963 is described by many Iraqis as a turning point in the modern history of Iraq. Within only one week of the coup, about three to five thousand communists and sympathizers with the Qassem government were arrested, tortured, and killed (Al-Ali 2007, 92).

Schools and sports grounds were transformed into concentration and interrogation camps. The scale of the violence and fear experienced in the immediate aftermath of the first Ba'th coup in 1963 is often referred to as a foretaste of what was to come during the Ba'th rule from 1968 to 2003. At the time, however, widespread resentment against the thuggish and brutal National Guard linked to the Ba'th party, as well as deep divisions within the party itself, eventually allowed the non-Ba'thist officer 'Abd Al-Salam 'Arif to install a military government in November, dissolve the National Guard, and arrest a number of leading Ba'thists (Abdullah 2003, 166).

In many accounts of the time, violence and repression receded dramatically once 'Arif managed to contain the Ba'th and especially the National Guard. Although dependent on the patronage and military support of President 'Arif, the civilian Prime Minister Al-Bazzaz tried to insure the respect of civil liberties and introduce some democratic structures into the state (Farouk-Sluglett and Sluglett 2003, 94).

The internal instability of the government increased when President Abdel Salam 'Arif died in a plane crash in 1966 and his less charismatic brother Abdel Rahman 'Arif took over as President. Regional developments also contributed to a weakening of the government: The Arab-Israeli war of 1967 left pro-Nasser Arab nationalists in disarray and on the defensive, strengthening the Ba'th camp of Arab nationalism. The Ba'th party had reorganized itself after the crackdown following the coup of 1963, allowing a faction controlled largely by members from Tikrit, a town northwest of Baghdad, to take control. In 1968, a second Ba'th coup paved the way for one of the most long-lasting and violent post World War II fascist regimes to emerge. It is during this period that Zubaida's lost love disappeared, the young pilot who grew up in the alley where Zubaida lived with her family and with whom she exchanged fleeting moments of eye contact and conversation.

One year after "the dictator" Saddam Hussein took over—when Hassan Al-Bakr, who had been President since the coup in 1968, stepped down in 1979—one of the bloodiest wars in the history of the region began. The war lasted eight years. For many Iraqi women who had not been involved in politics, the year 1980 marked a turning point in their own histories and the history of their country, the beginning of a series of bloody wars, violence, and hardship.

Zubaida remembers the war, which she calls, "the First War." Her younger brother was one of the tens of thousands of young men who were forced to fight in a war they did not believe in. When she last saw him before leaving the country, he was only a boy. The child of her family. And the family is secretive about his fate. Many years after his death at the front she receives a letter implying that he is dead.

Experiences of the Iran-Iraq war vary greatly. Overall, Iraqi women tend to stress that, despite hardships, life was still more bearable during this war than any of the subsequent wars in 1991 and 2003. Middle-class families in cities located far from the actual front in the south experienced relatively minor disruption to their daily lives. Yet, most Baghdadi women I talked to distinctly remembered the first days of the war as particularly traumatic, since they experienced air raids and missiles for the first time in the capital. Most Iraqi women also recalled having lost someone dear to them, if not a son, brother, father, or husband, then a cousin, a neighbor, or family friend. Women living closer to the front in the south experienced many more hardships during the Iran-Iraq war.

Despite a degree of discontent with the regime and also some level of sectarianism as a result of discriminations before and during the Ba'th regime, Iraqi Shi'i did not call for a merger with Iran or for self-rule in the south. Rather, most Iraqi Shi'i continued to stress their Arab identity and allegiance to the Iraqi nation, although not necessarily to the Iraqi regime. Saddam Hussein, on the other hand, continued to fear the lack of loyalty of the Shi'i population and collectively punished hundreds of thousands by forcibly deporting them to Iran. During the late-1970s, about 250,000 Iraqis of "Persian descent" were deported and their property confiscated. The deportations were stepped up at the beginning of the Iran-Iraq war. During the first year alone about 40,000 Iraqi Shi'i were forced to leave their homes, and in the course of the eight years of the war, an estimated 400,000 Iraqis ended up in Iran (Abdullah 2003; Tripp 2000).

Early in the novel, Zubaida experiences mixed feelings as she witnesses the destruction of Iraq on her television screen. She is angry and saddened by the sight of American soldiers destroying her home country and killing Iraqi soldiers. Is there "a missing truth"? Many Iraqis, like Zubaida, have been wondering whether there exists a plan to destroy Iraq and its rich history. Throughout the novel, it becomes evident that Zubaida distances herself from all political parties and is particularly critical of members of the Communist Party who come to visit her in East Germany. Like many former Iraqis who had either been members or sympathizers of the Iraqi Communist Party,

Zubaida is clearly disillusioned and holds the party responsible for the destruction of her home country, since elements of the party were supportive of the invasion.

Yet, Zubaida also thinks about previous waves of destruction and the human rights atrocities committed by the previous regime. People were arrested, tortured, and killed, whatever their ethnic or religious background, including Sunni Arabs in opposition to the regime. In addition to the suffering and forced deportation of Iraqi Shi'i, Zubaida also remembers the suffering of Iraqi Kurds. The most known element of a systematic repression and killing of Kurds was the 1987–1988 *Anfal* campaign, nominally a counterinsurgency operation, but in reality a carefully planned and executed program of ethnic cleansing in which 50,000 to 200,000 people are estimated to have been killed, most of them men and adolescent boys.[3] Thousands of Kurdish villages were systematically destroyed, and over a million and a half of their inhabitants deported to camps with no water, electricity, or sewage. Others were executed on the way out of their villages.

Under the leadership of Ali Hassan Al-Majid, a cousin of Saddam Hussein, the *Anfal* campaign has been particularly associated with the use of such chemical weapons as mustard and nerve gas. One of the most notorious attacks took place in the city of Halabja on March 16, 1988. Approximately 5,000 civilians died on that day alone and thousands suffered horrendous injuries. Many people were covered with horrible skin eruptions; others went blind and suffered severe neurological damage. Long-term effects have included various forms of cancer, infertility, and congenital diseases.

For decades, Iraq has not only existed inside the territorial boundaries of the nation state, but has also stayed alive within the numerous migrant and exile communities dispersed throughout the world. Iraq has been living in the hearts of Iraqis in diaspora; Iraq fills their imaginations. Alienation, nostalgia, and depression are chronic and widespread among Iraqis abroad, whether living in one of the neighboring countries in the Middle East, or farther away, in Europe, the Americas, Australia, or the Far East. Speaking to them, one often senses a great sadness. Yet, Iraqi communities in diaspora have also been great sources of hope, of political mobilization, of humanitarian and financial assistance, as well as creative synergies (Al-Ali 2007, 14).

Iraqi women and men have been leaving in significant numbers since the 1940s for a variety of different reasons. The vast majority had to leave because of political repression or fear of persecution. Others left to escape war and destruction. Still others sought educational and economic opportunities. During the period of economic sanctions (from 1990 to 2003), simple categories of voluntary versus forced migration blurred as thousands of Iraqis left in the context of a severe economic crisis and ongoing political repression.

Iraqis can be found in almost every country in the world today. The majority of Iraqi refugees live in neighboring countries, especially Iran, Jordan, Turkey, and Syria. There are also considerable Iraqi communities in Yemen, Lebanon, and the Gulf States. Although the bulk of Iraqis found asylum in Iran, in 2000, Iraqis were the second largest group of asylum applicants to the main industrialized countries (Chatelard 2002, 1). In Western Europe, Iraqis live chiefly in the United Kingdom, Germany, the Netherlands, and Sweden. In the United States, Iraqis are scattered throughout the country, but considerable communities can be found in Detroit, Chicago, Nashville, Los Angeles, and San Diego. The Iraqi dispersion has also extended to Canada, Australia, New Zealand, Indonesia, and Malaysia.

From the late-1950s onward, economic migrants and students were joined by political exiles. Many Iraqis who had been part of the elite associated with the monarchy left after the revolution in 1958. Later on, mainly communists fled the persecution, arrests and executions by Ba'this following the coups in 1963 and 1968. Throughout the Ba'th period (from 1968 to 2003), male and female opposition activists of all ethnic and religious backgrounds and across the political spectrum, including communists, Nasserites, democrats, and Islamists, had to flee from government repression.

Throughout the 1990s and the first three years of the twenty-first century, Iraqis migrated due to a mixture of economic and political factors (Chatelard 2002, 1). Many Iraqi refugees and asylum seekers who are living abroad today left Iraq during or after the Gulf war in 1991. Mainly Iraqi Kurds and Shi'i escaped after their failed uprisings against the regime of Saddam Hussein in 1991. The drainage of the marshlands in the south worsened the general hardships and repressions endured by the Marsh Arabs and led to more dispersals, especially to Iran. Displacement and forced resettlement were elements of the regime's strategy to undermine political opposition, to punish and subdue the Marsh Arabs, and to secure valuable economic resources.

Thirteen years of the most comprehensive sanctions system ever imposed on a country led to a deterioration in economic conditions and a humanitarian crisis. During and in the aftermath of the invasion in 2003, there has been an ongoing flow of people escaping the rampant violence, general lack of security, kidnappings, targeted assassinations of doctors and academics, a worsening humanitarian crisis, and deteriorating infrastructure. Over two million people have fled the country since 2004, raising the number of Iraqis abroad to over six million, more than a quarter of Iraqis in the world.

Thus, Iqbal Al-Qazwini finds herself in the company of a growing number of Iraqi women writers in exile, including Betool El-Khadairy, Alia Mamdouh, Haifa Zangana, and Buthaina Al-Naseri. Haifa Zangana eloquently depicts the characteristics of a new generation of Iraqi writers who have emerged in exile since the 1980s:

> Writing in exile is characterized by the dominance of memory; uprooted from one's country, the writer relies on memory as a vital tool, enabling him or her to recreate everything that happened in the past and preserve it intact. Memory extends to the present and may overshadow the future. For some, memory becomes life itself. Other writers are happy merely to visit it, using it to reflect on their bitter experiences in Iraq. In their first novels, mostly based on memory, they depict their personal experiences, addressing themes such as serving in the army, wars, imprisonment, fear, and the struggle to escape the country. (Zangana 2007, xiv)

Like many first novels by Arab women writers, Iqbal Al-Qazwni's novel contains autobiographical elements. Interwoven are stories based on the experiences of the author's friends and acquaintances. "In a way Zubaida's story is the story of my generation," Al-Qazwini has told me. Experiences of despair, alienation, and death in exile are common among men and women of her generation.

The specific setting of Zubaida's exile—in Berlin—provides an interesting insight into socialist contexts and post-socialist developments. Like many Iraqis on the political left, and other intellectuals and Iraqis from previously colonized countries, Zubaida experiences a great sense of disappointment and disillusionment when arriving in the former German Democratic Republic. There she finds a large disparity between her expectations of social justice and egalitarian values and the reality of an oppressive authoritarian regime which forbids or stifles self-expression.

Self-expression lies at the core of Zubaida's inner world, although she lacks the ability to interact expressively with people. Language becomes key to understanding her stream of thought, memories, and emotions. The English translation of the Arabic original leaves the reader with a taste for the idiosyncrasies of the Arabic language. Rich in metaphors and poetic, it is not always easily accessible for a Western reader. In the novel, Al-Qazwini's use of language evokes Zubaida's sense of alienation and estrangement. She is a stranger except in her imaginary travels to Arabic countries.

Historically, the novel ends after the downfall of the Ba'th regime in 2003, when Al-Qazwini constructs the last moments of the dictatorship in great detail. Some of this account has been documented, some of it imagined by the author. In the course of the novel, Zubaida loses her only very close friend, "The Warbling Nightingale," who most likely commits suicide. Al-Qazwini also leaves open the disappearance of another friend, a painter who leaves her in his studio studying his painting of a horse who has lost his rider and who sadly returns to his family. Living in an atmosphere of despair and grief, Zubaida appears to give up. Her heart beats become irregular. At the very end, while a reader may be left wondering whether Zubaida is suffering from a heart attack—and without recourse to medical attention—hope glimmers as Zubaida calmly falls asleep. Most Iraqis nowadays would like to fall asleep and wake up to a different reality. Perhaps Al-Qazwini is suggesting that this different reality needs to be constructed from within, since the physical reality is too hard to bear.

Nadje Al-Ali
December 2007
Centre for Gender Studies, SOAS, University of London

NOTES

1. Quotations from Al-Qazwini, unless otherwise noted, are from personal telephone and email conversations with the author during the fall of 2007.

2. Mandaeans (Sabaeans) are often described as those believing in the "teachings of John the Baptist." However, Mandaeans, who refer to themselves as following "the religion of Adam," have their own scriptures containing an account of John the Baptist which disagrees with much of the Christian Bible's depiction of him.

3. For more details, see Human Rights Watch (1993) and http://www. womenwarpeace.org/.

WORKS CITED

Al-Ali, Nadje. 2007. *Iraqi Women: Untold Stories from 1948 to the Present.* London and New York: Zed Books.

Al-Rasheed, Madawi. 1994. "The Myth of Return: Iraqi Arab and Assyrian Refugees in London." *Journal of Refugee Studies,* 7(2/3):199–219.

Abdullah, Thabit. 2003. *A Short History of Iraq: From 636 to the Present.* London: Pearson Longman.

Chatelard, Geraldine. 2002. "Jordan as a Transit Country: Semi-Protectionist Immigration Policies and Their Effects on Iraqi Forced Migrants." Working paper No. 61, New Issues in Refugee Research. Geneva: UNHCR.

Farouk-Sluglett, Marion, and Peter Sluglett. 2003. *Iraq Since 1958: From Revolution to Dictatorship, Fourth Edition.* London and New York: I.B. Tauris.

Human Rights Watch. 1993. *Genocide in Iraq: The Anfal Campaign Against the Kurds, A Middle East Watch Report.* New York, Washington, Los Angeles, London: Human Rights Watch.

Tripp, Charles. 2000. *A History of Iraq.* Cambridge: Cambridge University Press.

Zangana, Haifa. 2007. *Women on a Journey: Between Baghdad and London.* Translated by Judy Cumberbatch. Austin: University of Texas Press.